WOMEN OF GLORY

*Last night he'd dreamed about
Callie—soft, lush, torrid dreams.*

Since his divorce, Ty had shied away from women.
Callie Donovan was reawakening him to his desires.

But the feelings went beyond the sexual, he realized.
There was some intangible, magical gift Callie gave
him simply by being herself. She was like the spring
sun, healing old wounds. And more than anything,
he wanted to explore this new experience.

Right now, however, he and Callie were caught in the
cross fire threatening her and her career. And it was
up to him to bring her safely through the storm.

Ty vowed he wouldn't let her down. He had to make
this work. No matter the odds, he just had to....

Dear Reader,

Welcome to Silhouette *Special Edition* . . . welcome to romance.

Last year I requested your opinions on the books that we publish. Thank you for the many thoughtful comments. Throughout the past months I've been sharing quotes from these letters with you. This seems very appropriate while we are in the midst of our THAT SPECIAL WOMAN! promotion, as each of our readers is a very special woman.

This month, our THAT SPECIAL WOMAN! is Lt. Callie Donovan, a woman whose military career is on the line. Lindsay McKenna brings you this story of determination and love in *Point of Departure*.

Also this month is *Forever* by Ginna Gray, another book in the BLAINES AND THE McCALLS OF CROCKETT, TEXAS series. Erica Spindler brings you *Magnolia Dawn*, the second book in her BLOSSOMS OF THE SOUTH series. And don't miss Sherryl Woods's *A Daring Vow* — a tie-in to her VOWS series — as well as stories from Andrea Edwards and Jean Ann Donathan.

I hope you enjoy this book, and all of the stories to come!

Sincerely,

Tara Gavin
Senior Editor

QUOTE OF THE MONTH:

"I have an MA in Humanities. I like to read funny and spirited stories. I really enjoy novels set in distinctive parts of the country with strong women and equally strong men. . . . Please continue to publish books that are delightful to read. Nothing is as much fun as finding a great story. I will continue to buy books that entertain and make me smile."

—T. Kanowith, Maryland

LINDSAY McKENNA

POINT OF DEPARTURE

Silhouette®

SPECIAL EDITION®

Published by Silhouette Books

America's Publisher of Contemporary Romance

To all service women who have
battled with sexual harassment.

 SILHOUETTE BOOKS

ISBN 0-373-09853-7

POINT OF DEPARTURE

Printed in U.S.A.

LINDSAY McKENNA

spent three years serving her country as a meteorologist in the U.S. Navy, so much of her knowledge comes from direct experience. In addition, she spends a great deal of time researching each book, whether it be at the Pentagon or at military bases, extensively interviewing key personnel.

Lindsay is also a pilot. She and her husband of fifteen years, both avid "rock hounds" and hikers, live in Arizona.

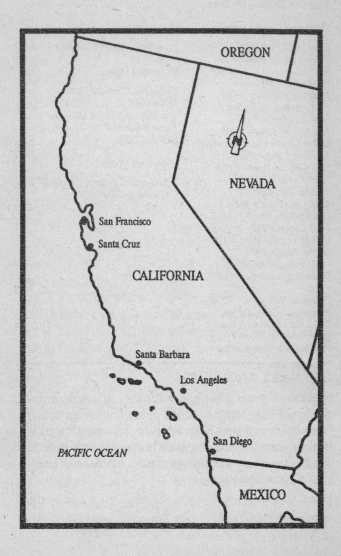

OREGON

NEVADA

San Francisco

Santa Cruz

CALIFORNIA

Santa Barbara

Los Angeles

San Diego

PACIFIC OCEAN

MEXICO

Chapter One

Lieutenant Callie Donovan wondered if it was a good idea to grab a quick dinner at the Officer's Club. Lately, with all the hubbub over the newspaper article about Callie and her sister Maggie coming to Miramar Naval Air Station—home of the cream of the naval aviation crop known as Top Guns—things had been going from bad to worse.

Callie frowned and pushed a lock of black hair off her forehead as she pulled into the Officer's Club parking lot. She'd already changed out of her summer uniform in the women's locker facility, and into a simple white, short-sleeved blouse, denim skirt and sandals. As she opened her car door, Callie laughed to herself, but the sound had a grim edge to it as she realized her carefully nondescript outfit was really more an attempt at camouflage than comfort.

Last Sunday's newspaper had featured a full-page profile on the Donovan sisters, under the auspices of "women challenging the male military bastion." Callie hadn't wanted to be interviewed, but effervescent Maggie, always happy to be in the forefront of leading women into male-dominated areas, had somehow talked her into it. Shutting the car door, Callie realized that it was Friday night, and the O Club parking lot was nearly full—mostly with vehicles of the young, eager pilots who attended Top Gun school. Again, she hesitated. The last place she wanted to be was on the firing line with a bunch of chauvinistic pilots angry about the newspaper article.

Callie's stomach rumbled. This was silly, she thought, impatiently smoothing her skirt. She needed to eat before driving to the local college to attend a still-life photography class, and the O Club was close and convenient. Shrugging off the intuitive warning, she slung her white purse across her shoulder and headed toward the club.

Day had turned to evening, but the dry desert heat lingered, and her blouse clung slightly to her damp skin. The light blue sky held a golden cast at the horizon. Although the Pacific Ocean was ten miles away, Callie caught a hint of saltiness on the air. In another hour, twilight would settle on the famous Southern California naval base and neighboring San Diego. Miramar was the aviation arm of the navy—and the most prestigious assignment Callie had ever been given. In her position as a satellite and photo interpreter, she'd always been hidden behind doors marked Top Secret, pouring over photos for hours, then issuing reports, never interfacing much with anyone but photographic intelligence staff. But Miramar was a different stripe of cat: there was always excitement at this station because the Top Guns trained here year round.

As she hurried across the asphalt, Callie saw many other young women heading for the club, mostly in groups of two and three. Her heart fell. These civilian women, dressed to the nines in snug skirts and high heels, were known as "groupies." On Friday and Saturday nights, the women swarmed to the O Club, openly courting the cocky young pilots by flirting, dancing and drinking with them.

Callie wanted none of the scene that generated so much excitement among the carrier pilots, who eagerly looked forward to the weekends. She never had. Naval aviators tended to be aggressive toward women, and usually had enough lines to sink a battleship—as she knew from hard-won experience. In four years, she'd fallen three times for navy pilots. And, as Maggie had informed her one day, she'd crashed and burned each time—sucked in with a line, her own damning naiveté paving the way to the end of the relationship.

Shaking her head, Callie slowed down and allowed the groups of civilian women to enter the O Club first. They would go to the bar, she knew, a huge area designed for heavy drinking, rowdy behavior, loud rock music and packed bodies. Callie, however, opened the door and entered the much-quieter dining room, adjacent to the bar. Here there was a lot less chance of being hit on by some drunk aviator.

Not that she'd be much of a target, anyway, she thought as the hostess led her toward a table at the rear of the spacious room. With her short hair, bland clothes and lack of makeup, Callie was hardly the type to attract the roving "wolf packs."

As Callie reached the small table, she recognized Lieutenant Andy Clark, who was assigned to Miramar as an Aggressor pilot—one of the men who trained the Top Gun candidates how to shoot to kill up in the sky. Seated two tables to her left, Andy looked up and nodded deferentially in her direction. Callie smiled and raised her hand in silent greeting before she sat down. Andy was married and the proud father of two little girls, she knew. His wife was a teacher, with the local school district, and they had a home in Bonsall, not far from the station.

Loud, irritating music drifted into the dining area, and with a sinking feeling, Callie realized that her table was easily viewed from the bar, which was packed, as usual, with aviators—in uniform to impress the multitude of circulating civilian women.

Games, she thought tiredly, as she sipped a glass of ice water. Callie hadn't known what games really were until she'd joined the navy, following in her sisters' footsteps. She'd learned fast, though, at Annapolis, where men had called her names, played dirty tricks on her, groped her and made her the object of their anger.

And the games hadn't stopped with her recent promotion to Miramar, Callie thought glumly after the waitress had taken her order for a hamburger and fries. Her new boss in the Intelligence section, Lieutenant Commander Hal Remington, had, since her arrival here a month ago, been more than a pest. Tall, darkly tanned and arrogant—and carrying the nickname "Honcho"—Remington embodied the stereotypical pilot image, making him a favorite of the groupies.

No, the games Remington played were barely disguised displays of hostility toward women. At first, coming to Miramar had looked like a wonderful feather in her career cap and the achievement of Callie's primary goal—job security. Transferring from the dark photographic rooms of the Pentagon to here, she'd felt like Persephone coming from the bowels of Hades to the topside of the world where there was sunshine, life and beauty.

Callie had earned her promotion. She'd paid her dues at the Pentagon, and her personnel jacket reflected her much-heralded abilities. But with Remington assigned as her immediate superior, Callie's joy at coming to Miramar had been quickly eclipsed. He was like a wolf on the prowl, harassing and intimidating the women in his section. Worse, he seemed to zero in on Callie with his insinuating remarks and barely veiled come-ons. But fear of losing her job, or at least getting bad marks in her personnel jacket, had kept her tight-lipped about the problem—even to Maggie.

Within twenty minutes her meal had arrived and Callie was glad. Although she tried not to show it, she was nervous. From time to time, out of the corner of her eye, she noticed some of the pilots at the bar pointing disparagingly in her direction. The entire station knew about the newspaper article, which, thanks largely to Maggie's outspokenness, had stirred up a lot of heated debate.

Why had she allowed Maggie to drag her into that interview? Callie thought for about the thousandth time since last Sunday. Not that she'd said much anyway. Maggie was so fiery and confident in comparison to Callie that the female reporter naturally had honed in on her. And for that, Callie was grateful. She concentrated on quickly eating her meal, mentally preparing for her upcoming class. Tonight she would be showing some photo techniques in the darkroom, and she wanted to get there a little early to look at her notes and doublecheck the equipment.

"Hey, sweet thing..."

Callie's heart took one gigantic bound, and a french fry halted halfway to her mouth. She'd recognize that grating voice anywhere. It was Lieutenant Commander Remington. Lifting her head, Callie firmly ordered herself not to react although fear sizzled through her gut, tightening it into a knot.

Remington smiled and lifted his hand in a sloppy salute. "You know, you could dress in a burlap bag and it wouldn't matter, Donovan," he said, his words slurring slightly. He weaved unsteadily and took a step back to peer down at her crossed legs. "Your legs have been driving me nuts all day. I'm glad you stopped by the O Club. It gives me another chance to look at them."

Callie gulped and saw that Remington's narrow blue eyes were hazed from alcohol. He was her superior. What should she do? Her heart was bounding like a rabbit's—a rabbit caught between the paws of a slavering wolf.

Maybe if she played along, tried teasing him back, it would make him go away, Callie thought. Attempting to smile, she set her food aside.

"Commander, I'm sure your wife has a very nice set of legs, too." Remington had just recently married for a third time, from what she understood.

He lurched forward and placed his hands flat on the white linen cloth of the table. Patches adorned each arm of his olive green one-piece flight suit, and his name was printed in gold on a black leather square above the left breast pocket. His mouth drew into a little-boy smile as he pinned her with his gaze. "Sweet cheeks, I still think you've got the best legs on the station, despite that asinine article I read last Sunday."

Inwardly, Callie winced. *The article.* The light in Remington's assessing gaze was neither kind nor friendly. No, she saw savagery linked with a hatred that made her blood chill. He was smiling, but the expression never reached his eyes. Callie felt trapped—there was no place to run.

"Look, Commander, I'm in a hurry. I've got a class to teach tonight—"

Reaching out, Remington grazed her cheek with his fingers. "Damn, you're a nice piece of flesh. Why did you have to side with your red-haired witch of a sister? Are you an ice queen like her?"

Paralyzed with fear, Callie allowed Remington to stroke her cheek for several seconds before she slowly pulled away. She felt heat flare up from her neck into her face. Blushing had always gotten her into trouble at Annapolis, she thought distractedly. Remington was her boss. She couldn't make a scene or he'd put low ratings in her personnel record, and the promised rank would be pulled from her. She couldn't overreact. Belatedly, Callie thought about what Maggie would have done: she'd have called him on his drunken behavior and insisted he leave. But Remington wasn't Maggie's boss....

Her mind whirling with options that might defuse Remington, Callie stammered, "My—my sister has her opinions. If you read the article, you probably noticed that I had very little to say about it. I'm not the pilot, she is.''

Remington slowly straightened, looked back to the bar and raised his hand. Two other aviators, obviously young Top Gun students, waved back, big grins on their faces. He smiled lopsidedly and placed his hands arrogantly on his hips.

''Honey, you got the same fighting blood in your veins. I don't care whether you're a pilot or not. You Donovans are nothing but man-hating Amazons. You think you're better than us, don't you?''

The pulse at Callie's throat was throbbing. She'd completely lost her appetite. She felt like a cornered animal beneath Remington's attack. In vain, she tried to smile again.

''Maggie is happily married, Commander. I don't think that classifies her as a man-hater, do you?''

With a snort, Remington leered at her. ''You know what, Donovan? You need a *real* man. You're skittish. You're distrustful. I can see it in your eyes. I see it at work. You don't like to be touched. You don't like men's attention at all, do you?'' His smile was deadly as he asked, ''What's the problem? Do you prefer the company of women over men?''

Callie gasped. Remington's voice was deep and carried a long way. Inwardly, she felt as if she were dying. She was sure that Lieutenant Clark could hear every word. This wasn't the way Callie wanted to start out three years of duty at Miramar. She knew what happened to women in the service when they got labeled; fair or not, the rumors followed them like a disease and could destroy their career.

With a brittle laugh, Callie sat back and held Remington's gloating look. "Commander, I think you've had a few too many drinks."

"That may be, honey," he said as he lurched toward her. "Are you a lesbian?" He held out his hand and touched her cheek again. "Maybe what you need is someone like me. You split tails are all alike. You need a little taming."

Callie froze again at Remington's touch. There was no end to this torture, to this horrible, escalating humiliation. The few other patrons in the dining room were far away and mostly couples. She didn't dare look in Andy's direction, too mortified to ask for help.

Moving away from his touch again, Callie whispered, "Commander, I have a class coming up in less than an hour. If you don't mind, I'd like to finish my meal."

Backing away, Remington grinned and flipped off a salute. "Sure, honey. You feed that beautiful brain of yours." He winked at her. "I'll take care of that hot property you call a body. Be seeing you around...."

Shattered, Callie shivered in terror and relief as Remington staggered back to the bar, toward his two young charges. Callie could see them slap him heartily on the back when he returned. Remington leaned over and said something, and all three broke out into raucous gales of laughter.

Thoroughly humiliated, Callie wanted nothing more than to get up and run out of the O Club as fast as her legs would carry her. But she thought of Maggie, who always accused her of running from showdowns. She'd run from them at Annapolis, too. There was no safe place. Callie knew from firsthand experience that knights on white horses no longer existed. There was such polarization between men and women in the military that the old ways were dead. Instead, Callie, like everyone else, was left floundering to find and establish new rules for dealing with the opposite gender.

After ten more minutes that felt like an eternity of forcing herself to nibble at her now-cold hamburger and fries, Callie decided she could leave. Her ears seemed keyed to Remington's harsh, loud laughter, which rose above the din of voices. Gripping her white shoulder bag, she made herself get up slowly, as if nothing was wrong—even though everything was wrong. Now Remington was harassing her off duty as well as at work. What was she going to do? What *could* she do?

As Callie walked out of the dining room and toward the main entrance, she knew that any complaint over Remington's head would be stonewalled. Remington was a "ring-knocker," an Annapolis graduate, just as she was. And so was Commander Ferris, their boss. "The brotherhood" was alive and well in the navy, and Callie was familiar with their code: they would never squeal on one another. If she complained that Remington was bothering her, Commander Ferris would conveniently hush up the whole thing—and her job ratings would go down.

No, no one who valued her job would dare take on the male-dominated navy, especially over this kind of unprovable harassment. Compressing her lips, Callie blindly headed out the door. The huge parking lot was packed with all models of cars, and twilight hovered across the Southern California landscape. The soft plop of her sandals mingled with the sounds of jets taking off at a nearby concrete airstrip. Sea gulls were always present here, and a few still winged across the parking lot, silent and graceful. The lights above the lot had already come on in response to the rapidly fading light, and Callie glanced at her watch: she had forty minutes to get to her class.

"Hey! Sweet thing!"

Callie gasped and whirled around at the sound of Remington's grating voice. She saw him hurrying toward her, the two other pilots in tow. No! If she didn't escape, Remington would make her life miserable. She hurried to her car. Her hand shaking badly, Callie dug in her purse for the keys.

"Hey!" Remington boomed out, closing the distance.

Unable to locate her keys, Callie stopped digging and turned coolly toward Remington and his buddies. They couldn't even walk a straight line, she noticed. They had to grip each other by the arm or shoulder. She saw a look of pure, unadulterated glee in Remington's shadowed features, and his predatory smile was chilling.

"What is it, Commander?" Callie demanded in her firmest, most unruffled tone. Maybe if she came across as being in charge, they'd back down and leave her alone. She gripped her purse, tense and wary as the three pilots came to a halt less than a foot away from her, effectively trapping her against the side of her car.

"I wanna know—" Remington's voice slurred as he reached out to slide his hand down her cheek, to her neck "—if you've got any fire in those icy veins of yours." He laughed harshly and glanced at his friends. "Now, Neil, here, says you're the original ice queen. My other buddy, Dale, says you're just like all the other split tails in the navy." He caressed her neck and then allowed his hand to trail provocatively down her shoulder and arm. "So which is it, honey? We gotta know."

Callie's eyes widened enormously as Remington's touch became shockingly intimate. As he draped his fingers down her arm, he deliberately brushed the side of her breast. With a small cry, Callie shrank against her car, its still-hot metal burning through her clothes.

"Leave me alone!" she begged hoarsely.

The second pilot, the blond called Dale, reached out and gripped her by the shoulder to stop her escape. "Hey, doll face, don't be hasty. I'm God's gift to women. Why would you want to run from me?" His mouth twisted into a snarl. "According to that article, you think you're just as good as me in *every* way."

Trapped, Callie tried to jerk out of Dale's grip. In doing so, she collided with Neil. She found herself pressed against his chest, and his long, strong arms wrapped around her waist. His hair was dark and his equally dark brown eyes narrowed with intensity.

"Hey, look at this, guys—the ice queen has fallen into my arms!" he crowed triumphantly. Leaning forward, he tried to kiss Callie. Dodging his attempt, she threw her hands upward.

"That's not nice," Neil muttered. "I'm wearing all the right clothes, I got a Corvette and Armani suits, honey. I'm just what you need...."

With another cry, much louder this time, Callie shoved him away. Wanting only to escape now, she realized she was in serious trouble. These pilots were drunk, and they were angry at her because of the article. Remington stepped on one of her sandals as she struggled, tearing the leather strap. The shoe fell aside, leaving Callie's nylon-clad foot defenseless against the blisteringly hot asphalt.

"Ow!" she cried, and tried to dodge Remington's outstretched hand.

"Bitch," he breathed savagely. Grabbing her by the arm, he jerked her toward him. "She's mine," he snarled to the other two pilots, who gripped her shoulders, holding her captive so that Remington could touch her.

Tears flooded into Callie's eyes as she saw his hand rise. Was he going to strike her? Wincing, one hand held up to her face, she tried to scream, but all that came out was a feeble, short-circuited shriek. In the next instant, Remington had jammed his hand inside her blouse, fumbling for and finding her breasts. She heard the other pilots laughing as they held her in a tight grip.

No! Callie focused on screaming as loud as she could. The pilots had her pinned against the car, and with their combined strength, it was impossible to escape. The groping of drunken hands across her breasts, hips and thighs sent a sheet of fear through her. Concentrating on her scream, she jerked out of one pilot's reach. As she made the quick movement, Callie lifted her leg, her knee connecting solidly with Remington's thigh.

Remington leaped back with a roar, and this time Callie's scream shattered the twilight. Thrown off balance as the other two pilots tried to reestablish their grips on her, she slammed backward onto the asphalt, roughly shredding the skin on her legs and knees as she rolled over to try and escape. Remington leaped forward and Callie screamed again as she lunged upward toward freedom. If she didn't, she knew he was going to rape her. The power of that fear pushed her to her feet, but the pilot's hand shoved full force into her chest, knocking her backward again.

Sharp pain shot up Callie's ankle as her foot twisted beneath her. Wouldn't this nightmare ever end? As she fell to the ground once more, she screamed a third time, but now her cry sounded like that of a frightened, beaten animal.

All three pilots crowded around her, reaching and groping, their laughter making her plight all the worse. Kicking out with her feet and hands, Callie sobbed, tears blurring her vision as she cried out for help again. The nightmare of Annapolis came crashing back. Once again she was being brutally attacked—and no help had come for her then, either.

Chapter Two

A woman screamed, her voice carrying through the stifling California-desert heat. Lieutenant Commander Ty Ballard stood by the open door of his sports car. He'd just had a beer at the O Club and was ready to leave. Another shriek drifted across the huge parking lot. Squinting in the twilight, Ty could barely make out the handful of pilots clustered around a compact car at the rear of the lot. To his left, he saw a group of young civilian women walking toward the O Club. Had one of them screamed? But Ty knew it couldn't have been. This had been a scream of terror. Gripping the frame of the door, he frowned as he scanned the lot again.

Still, how many times had he heard shrieks and squeals out here? On Friday and Saturday nights the pilots and groupies partied to all hours—inside the club and outside in the parking lot—and to say they

were boisterous was putting it mildly. Ty lifted his chin
and tried to evaluate the direction from which the
scream had come. His frown deepening, he slowly
closed the door, his gaze locked again on the spot, almost a quarter mile away, where the group of pilots
huddled near the small car.

It wasn't any of his business. Often he'd seen a pilot and a civilian woman tussling playfully in the
parking lot—only to move into a passionate embrace
and torrid kiss. Sometimes it seemed as if they were
fighting at first. Sometimes they were, Ty admitted,
and he didn't get involved in the fracas. Soon they'd
be making up just as passionately. Slowly, he moved
around his car and started walking toward the end of
the parking lot. He felt foolish. It was probably just a
girl or girls having fun with a bunch of drunken pilots. If he came barging in, they'd all tell him to get
lost. Still dressed in the day's uniform, his one-piece
green flight suit, Ty ruefully rubbed the back of his
neck as he hesitantly moved forward.

The abject fear in the third scream sent a chill down
Ty's spine and made the hair on the back of his neck
stand up. The sound could no longer be confused with
youthful hijinks. He broke into a trot, weaving among
the parked cars. The twilight offered only poor visi-
bility and he couldn't quite make out who the pilots
were, or where the woman was. He could see what
appeared to be a lot of shoving and pushing going on
around the car.

As he drew closer, Ty recognized two of the pilots
from the class he taught at the Top Gun facility, lieutenants Neil Thorson and Dale Oakley. Thanks to his
daily five-mile run, Ty was breathing easily as he approached the group—and recognized a fellow officer

of same rank, Hal Remington. Ty felt a sudden sense of dread. Remington was a known stalker of anything in heels. Although he was married, he made no bones about keeping score of how many females he'd bedded. In fact, he displayed a gun holster in his office, with red, wooden bullets in the leather loops to announce to his fellow officers how many women he'd laid.

Ty's concern shifted to the woman jammed up against the car by the pilots' bodies. He couldn't get a good look at her—only enough to see that she was in civilian clothing, probably a groupie. Again he heard her shriek and then sob as she struggled to escape the groping hands.

"Hey!" he snarled, gripping Remington's broad shoulder. "Ease off!"

Remington whirled around, throwing his arm up in reaction and knocking Ballard's hand away. "Get lost," he growled.

The woman fell to the asphalt, and Ty elbowed his way between the hard-breathing pilots, forcing them back from where she lay. He glared at Thorson and Oakley.

"Enough!" he ordered. Then he whirled around to face Remington, who was glaring malevolently at him. "Commander, what's this all about?"

Remington wiped his mouth with the back of his hand. "Ballard. I might have known it would be you." He thrust his hand toward the woman. "This is my woman—go get your own. She's *my* property."

Ty gripped Remington's arm as the man pushed toward her. The sound of her sobbing assured him that this wasn't a game, and that she wasn't enjoying it.

The smell of liquor on Remington's breath was over-whelming. "Leave her alone."

"Screw you, Ballard. She's mine! She asked for this."

Ty held on to Remington's arm and glanced behind him at the woman, who sat on the asphalt, her hands pressed against her face. "She's not anyone's property," he said through gritted teeth, giving Remington a shove backward. Glancing at the two lieutenants, who had backed off and were looking a bit guilty, Ty added, "Get the hell out of here. Now."

"Yes, sir!" Thorson said thickly, trying to rear-range his flight suit.

"Yes, sir," Oakley added, with just a trace of sar-casm.

Remington jerked out of Ty's grip. "Get away, Ballard. This woman asked for it. She's a tease. And this time she isn't getting off so lucky. She wants it. She wants me."

Not trusting Remington, Ty remained where he stood. "I don't care what she asked for, she's not en-joying your attack, Remington. Why don't you leave her alone?"

Smirking, Remington glared down at the woman. "Bitch," he spat. "Maybe you'll think twice before you go around proclaiming women are the second coming." He raised his head and pinned his dark gaze on Ty. "You did a stupid thing coming out here and breaking up our fun, Ballard."

Ty tensed, wondering if Remington was going to throw a punch at him. The woman's sobs had soft-ened, but there was no doubt she'd been hurt in the scuffle. "Take off," he told Remington. "Go get a drink and cool off, or better yet, go home to your wife."

His mouth lifting in a snarl, Remington retreated and placed his cap on his head. "You're one to talk, Ballard. Your ex-wife was smart to drop you." He grinned a little, his arrogance back in place. "Hell, you can't even keep a woman."

"That's enough."

Flipping Ballard a salute, Remington turned and walked unsteadily back toward the Officer's Club.

Ty turned around. Darkness was following on the heels of twilight, hiding the woman's features as he crouched over her.

"It's okay," he murmured, and reached out to put a comforting hand on her small, shaking shoulder. Instantly, her hands flew away from her face as she shrank from his touch. Ty's eyes widened and he froze in shock.

"Lieutenant Donovan?" he croaked in disbelief. "Is that you?"

Callie nodded and tried to wipe the tears from her eyes. "Y-yes."

"Oh, God," Ty muttered. He reached into his back pocket and withdrew a linen handkerchief. "I'm sorry. Here, take this. I thought you were a groupie...." Quickly, he began to assess her condition. The front of her blouse had been ripped open, exposing part of her white cotton bra. Her hands, elbows and knees were covered with numerous bloody scrapes. She was trembling badly, and her blue eyes looked huge and shocked. Because of his duties as an instructor, Ty knew about Callie Donovan coming on board Miramar about a month ago, although they'd never been officially introduced. He'd read the Sunday newspaper, though, and he recognized her from the photo.

"Are you all right?" he asked, again placing his hand on her shoulder. There was such devastation in her eyes that he automatically tightened his grip. For a year now, Ty had been in a no-man's-land of emotional deprivation, but now, searching her face, he felt his heart squeeze in response to her suffering. Caught off guard, Ty could only lean down, lost in the luminous blue of her eyes.

"Y-yes, I'm fine," Callie quavered. "Fine..." Ensnared by the officer's penetrating gray gaze, Callie felt paralyzed. She was just beginning to feel the smarting pain of the scrapes that covered her palms and legs. She tore her gaze from his, the handkerchief fluttering nervously in her hands as she dabbed at her bloody knees. Her heart refused to settle down, and she gulped back tears, longing to howl like a wounded animal.

"No, I don't think you are all right," Ty whispered more firmly. "I'm Lieutenant Commander Ty Ballard. I was coming out of the O Club when I heard you scream." As Ty gazed down at her long legs, he noticed that one foot was without a sandal, and he could see swelling around the ankle. "What the hell was going on? Why did Remington and those jerks attack you?" he demanded, his voice tightening with anger. Remington was Callie Donovan's boss in the Intelligence section—what did he think he was doing?

Sniffing, Callie looked up at the pilot. Commander Ballard had a strong, narrow face with glittering gray eyes that missed nothing. He wasn't heavily muscled. Instead he possessed the lean, catlike body that so many pilots had because of the severe demands flying made on them. He looked like a hunter in every nuance of the word, from his eyes, which assessed her minutely, to the thinning of his mouth into a line that spoke volumes about his real feelings.

His almost-predatory look belied the gentle touch of his spare fingers, draped across her shoulder in a comforting gesture. Callie opened her mouth to speak, but a huge lump formed in her throat, and all she could do was stare up at him. She hadn't expected help, yet she'd gotten it—in the form of another pilot. But experience told her that pilots in any form were trouble.

"I—I'm really okay, Commander Ballard." Feeling humiliated, Callie started to push herself up from her sitting position on the asphalt. Instantly, he was there, both hands beneath her arms to help her stand. He was strong without being hurting or forceful, Callie noticed, almost unwillingly. As she put weight on her right foot, pain shot through her ankle.

Callie uttered a small cry and closed her eyes in reaction—and found herself swept into Ballard's arms as she crumpled helplessly against his tall, lean form. Her face pressed to the rough cotton of his flight uniform, she placed her palm against his chest in an effort to stand on her own, although something deep within her begged, just for a moment, to simply hide within his strong, protective embrace.

"Easy," Ty whispered, his mouth very close to her ear, "just take it easy." Her black hair felt thick and silky beneath his lips, and he inhaled the subtle fragrance of her faint, spicy perfume. "You need a doctor," he said, his hands cupping her shoulders to ensure she wouldn't lose her balance and fall.

"N-no, I don't. Please, just let me get in my car and I'll go home." Panic gripped Callie, but she couldn't force herself to leave the harbor of Ballard's care.

Shaking his head, Ty saw her take all the weight off her right foot, which had swollen nearly to the size of a grapefruit. "Listen, you might have torn muscles in that ankle of yours. Let me help you to my car, and I'll take you over to the dispensary. Besides, you need to get these scrapes and cuts tended to. They're still bleeding."

Dazed, Callie watched as he gently opened her hand and displayed her palm so that she could see the damage for herself. She remembered vaguely feeling the bite of the asphalt into her flesh when she'd fallen the first time. Now her hands and knees throbbed unremittingly. "Well, I—"

Ty grimly moved around and picked up her purse, tossed aside during the melee. Keeping one hand on her, because she was none too steady, he slung the purse across his shoulder and smiled a bit. "Hold on. You're going for a ride, Lieutenant."

Callie opened her mouth to protest, but to no avail. In one smooth motion, Ballard lifted her off her feet and brought her against him as if she didn't weigh more than a feather. Automatically, Callie placed her arms around his neck.

The firmness of his arms around her made her release a held breath. The strength of him as a man was all too real, but in the sense of security, not brutality. He was much stronger than he looked upon first glance. "You don't have to carry me—"

"I know, I know." Ty tried to keep the pleasure out of his voice. When had a woman felt so good in his arms? And then, sourly, he reminded himself that he'd been without any woman since the divorce. Still, Ty couldn't quite recall when a female had fitted so well against him.

Ballard's low voice soothed Callie's shattered emotions, and she drew in a ragged breath as she relaxed in his arms. "Th-thank you..." Wearily, she rested her head against his shoulder. For a moment, she felt his arms tighten around her, and all the tension fled from her as she capitulated completely to his strength.

"I'm just sorry I didn't get there sooner." Ty liked her melodic, breathy voice with just a hint of depth. Wildly aware of her head next to his, her arms around him, he managed a one-cornered smile. "Hell of a way to meet, isn't it? I'm an instructor over at Top Gun. You're Maggie Donovan's younger sister, aren't you?"

"Yes," she murmured, suddenly feeling very tired and very old. "I shipped out to Miramar a month ago."

"I thought so. Intelligence section, right?"

"Yes." Callie tried to sound as if she were fine, but she wasn't. Her past seemed to be hanging like some terrible mirror in front of her. Annapolis had been a special kind of hell—things had happened there that she'd never even told Maggie or her other sisters, Caitlin and Alanna. All four Donovan women had gone through their respective academies, but Callie had never shared the terrible torment she'd endured.

Ty didn't really want to release Callie, but as he approached his black sports car, he reluctantly lowered her to the pavement. Supporting her with one hand and unlocking the door with the other, he ushered her into the plush leather interior. Despite the darkness, he could see that she had a heart-shaped face and huge blue eyes that were shadowed with fear.

Smiling reassuringly at her, Ty slid into the driver's seat and started the engine. Callie was leaning back against the seat, her lips slightly parted, the bloody white linen handkerchief knotted tightly between her hands, resting in the lap of her denim skirt. "Here," he said, "let me help you with the seat belt," and he leaned over and pulled it across her, snapping it into place.

Wearily, Callie looked up at him through her lashes. "Thanks... Normally, I'm not so helpless."

After snapping on his own seat belt, Ty guided the car out of the parking lot. "There are times when you need to lean on someone else," he told her quietly. But hadn't his ex-wife, Jackie, accused him of never being there for her, that she'd never had him to lean on when she desperately wanted his support? After a hellish year of living through their painful divorce, Ty had had to face facts: he wasn't very good husband material. Maybe now, in some small way, he might atone for his failure to be there for Jackie by being here for Callie Donovan.

It took less than ten minutes to get to the dispensary, which sat near the Top Gun facility at the station. As Ty helped Callie from the car, he noticed how pale she was.

"Let me walk," she pleaded. "Don't carry me in. It's too embarrassing."

He shut the car door and tried to smile. "So, knights on white horses are dead, are they?"

Callie stood in the circle of his right arm, his hand around her waist. Ty was tall compared to her five-foot-five-inch frame. She could see a wry quality in his gray eyes, darkly shadowed by some unknown emotion, and she heard self-mockery in his husky voice.

Despite her own shock, she sensed that he, too, bore emotional wounds from his past. "You were a knight," she whispered. "You rescued me. I thought I was going to be raped by them. I didn't expect to get help. Not here. Not these days...."

Her words chilled Ty to the bone. He nodded and gently nudged her to begin making her slow, limping way to the dispensary door. "Remington's a bastard, but I don't think he'd rape you. He was drunk."

Callie shot him a look. "Drunk or not, that's no excuse for them attacking me."

The quaver of real fury in her voice stirred Ty. "I'm not defending them," he said softly. "What they did was wrong."

The bright lights momentarily blinded Callie. She didn't really want to be here. She wanted to curl up at home, left alone to nurse her wounds. After all, that's what she'd always done—take care of herself by herself. Now here was Ballard, solicitous and sensitive to her needs, and she had no idea how to react to him. Long ago, she'd lumped navy pilots under one simple description: arrogant, insensitive, egotistical and selfish. And no man had forced her to challenge that characterization—until now. As she limped down the green-and-white-tiled passageway toward the nursing station, Callie tried to grip the torn edges of her blouse with her hand, embarrassed by how she must look to the corpswaves and nurses.

The nurse on duty took her name and wrote everything down. Then she led her to a cubicle formed from three white sheets, where, with Ballard's help, Callie was able to sit up on the gurney to await the arrival of the doctor on duty. This close to Ballard, she couldn't escape the anger banked in his eyes, and she wondered who it was for. Her? Or the pilots? She knew from painful experience that pilots stuck together, bonded tighter than glue under any perceived attack by an outsider.

Still, if Ballard was angry with her, or blaming her for what had happened, why was he still here with her? Moistening her lips, Callie glanced at him, standing stoically beside the gurney.

"You don't have to stay, Commander. I'll be okay now," she managed to say, her heart squeezing oddly in her chest. She had to pull herself together!

Ty raised his head and settled his gaze on Callie. "How will you get back to your car?" Beneath the fluorescent lights overhead, she looked very pale, her skin appearing translucent under the harsh glare. Her hair was in disarray, and Ty suddenly was seized with the most maddening urge to gently tunnel his fingers through that black, shiny mass and tame it all back into order. The impulse was as crazy as it was unexpected, and Ty jammed his hands deep into his pockets. Although Callie was an officer, she didn't have that outer toughness so many of the women seemed to wear as armor in the male-dominated military world.

Callie inwardly railed at Ty's response. He could have said "I want to stay because you need help." No, he was only concerned with his responsibility to get her back to her car. Now that the incident had passed, no doubt he'd take the side of Remington and his brother pilots. Trying to stop the aching hurt in her chest, she merely nodded and looked away. But why should she be hurt or affected by this man? Her emotions in utter disarray, Callie had no easy answers.

"Hi," a tall woman in her forties said, pushing aside one of the sheet dividers, "I'm Dr. Rose Lipinski, duty physician. Looks like you took a few bumps and bruises, Lieutenant Donovan.''

Callie was thankful the doctor was a woman. A part of her relaxed as the redheaded Dr. Lipinski came forward to examine her. The doctor was lean as a rail, but her green eyes sparkled with warmth.

''I guess I do look a little beat up,'' she said, automatically reaching to shake hands with the doctor. At the sight of her bloody, lacerated palm, she gave the doctor an apologetic look and pulled it back.

Lipinski smiled understandingly. ''What happened, Ms. Donovan?'' she asked, as she gently began to examine Callie's hands, knees and the swollen right ankle.

''I was accosted in the O Club parking lot,'' Callie whispered, her throat suddenly closing with tears. Embarrassed, she raised her hand to wipe the threatening moisture from her eyes. She saw Dr. Lipinski's own eyes narrow speculatively as she continued her examination.

''Attacked,'' Ballard growled.

The doctor stopped her examination, twisted to look over her shoulder and studied him in silence. ''Really? And who are you?''

''Ty Ballard.''

''Oh, yes, I've heard of you.... Top Gun, right?''

''Yes, an instructor.''

''Did you see Ms. Donovan being attacked, Commander?''

Ty nodded. ''I was walking to my car after a beer at the O Club when I heard her scream.''

''I see.'' Rose studied Callie's drawn features. ''You know the man who did this to you?''

"Men," Ty corrected grimly, moving within a foot of the two women. "Three men."

The doctor's thin brows drew downward with censure. She turned and picked up some gauze from the nearby sink and methodically began to clean Callie's hands and knees. "Can you identify them?" she asked quietly.

Callie nodded. "Yes." She shrugged. "One is my boss, Lieutenant Commander Remington. The other two are Top Gun students."

"Lieutenants Thorson and Oakley," Ty provided darkly. "Both are TAD fighter pilots from the *Enterprise.* They're at the top of their class so far, fighting it out for first place." He scowled. "They've got real killer instincts."

Callie felt a chill run through her. "That's a good description of them," she choked out.

"Oh?" Dr. Lipinski swabbed Callie's palms with an antiseptic that stained her skin an orange color. "And how would you describe them, Ms. Donovan?"

Suddenly uncomfortable at the tension in the doctor's voice, Callie murmured, "Drunk, arrogant and violent."

"I see...." Dr. Lipinski carefully examined the swollen ankle. "Looks like a good sprain, Ms. Donovan. Does it hurt if I turn it this way? That?"

Callie withstood the jagged pain as the other woman gently moved the ankle in every conceivable direction. She was trying to be a good patient, but between Ballard's angry intensity and Lipinski's bird doglike snooping, she longed to escape.

"So," the doctor continued in a low voice as she wrapped Callie's ankle in an Ace bandage, "you saw the whole thing, Commander?"

Ty shrugged. "I saw part of it, Doc."

"Were they all drunk?" she asked.

"Yes, they were. I could smell the liquor on their breath."

"Boys will be boys, eh?" the doctor murmured, her frown deepening. As she finished wrapping Callie's ankle, she smiled up at her. "I want you to tell me what happened from beginning to end, Ms. Donovan. I'll need the information for my report." She reached over to the counter and picked up a metal clipboard and pen.

Shifting uncomfortably on the gurney, Callie said, "I don't think this is necessary, Doctor. All I want to do is go home and rest. I'm very tired. Exhausted, if you want the truth."

"I understand," Dr. Lipinski said soothingly as she rested her hip against the gurney. "But this is a serious offense, and I've got to report it."

Callie's mouth dropped open, and she stared at the grim-faced doctor, whose pen was poised above the form. "What do you mean, report it?"

"Lieutenant, at the least, you've been sexually harassed. At worst, the shore-patrol officials would say you've been assaulted. Now, I'm legally bound to report this kind of thing. If I don't, I'm in hot water. Besides, these pilots think they're a gift to women and I'm sick and tired of seeing these kinds of cases come through my doors. It's time that it stopped."

Her heart pounding, Callie stammered, "B-but I don't want this reported! Doctor, I have a career to think about. It was my *boss* that did this to me! I'm up for an early promotion to lieutenant commander, and I don't want to lose it. You can't report this!"

Lipinski's lean face softened slightly. "I'm sorry, Ms. Donovan. I have to do my duty, and you, more than most, should understand that. I have to note your injuries, the fact that your blouse has been torn. I have to provide a written report of your abrasions and the presence of several red marks on your chest between your breasts from their groping." She shook her head adamantly. "Believe me, this is best."

"For who?" Callie cried, her voice cracking. Wildly, she looked to Ballard for support. He stood, dark faced, his arms folded tightly across his chest, his eyes filled with anger. Probably at her—or the doctor? She wasn't sure which.

"For you," Lipinski said calmly, beginning to fill out the form. "And for every woman on or off this station who is sexually harassed by men who think they can keep getting away with it. Well, they can't."

Panic spread through Callie and she gripped the doctor's arm. "Please, you can't do this! I don't want to press charges against them! I just want to drop it and let it go. My career is more important to me than this!"

Dr. Lipinski lifted her chin, her eyes assessing. "Lieutenant, it isn't a matter of whether you want to press charges or not. I'm bound by law to report this to the shore patrol and the legal department. And I'm tired of seeing women coming in here too frightened to testify before either a civil court or a navy board of investigation. Don't worry, you'll have me as a corroborating witness."

"That isn't going to help me and you know it!" Callie rasped. "My career will be ruined! The navy will slot me into some dead-end job and then force me to resign. I've seen it done too many times. You can't do this to me, Dr. Lipinski!"

Ty moved forward, his hand coming to rest on Callie's tense shoulder. "The doctor doesn't have a choice, Callie," he offered, trying to soothe her.

Angrily, Callie shrugged his hand off her shoulder. Filled with a fear that made her more vocal than usual, she insisted, "Commander, that's easy for you to say. You're a man in a man's world."

Ty retreated, realizing that Callie was right. He saw the tears in her luminous eyes and wanted somehow to comfort her. But there was no comfort. "I can't deny it," he murmured apologetically.

"You'll see the wisdom of this," the doctor said gently, "after you get over the shock of being attacked, Ms. Donovan. Right now your senses are heightened, along with your feelings. I understand your concerns, but if women don't stand up and fight back, more women are going to be hurt. Do you want that?"

Breathing hard, Callie wiped the tears from her cheeks. "My sister Maggie is just like you," she answered angrily. "But I'm not like her, and I'm not like you! If this gets reported, my career is gone! Finished!"

"Lieutenant Maggie Donovan has been very influential," Lipinski murmured, continuing to fill out the forms. "I admire her very much. She's done a lot to help women in the military be seen as equals."

Callie felt the doctor's gaze, felt the accusation in her voice at Callie's weak stance. Well, that was too bad, because she didn't have Maggie's guts. All her early confidence had been taken from her back in her plebe year at Annapolis. Once she'd been the kind of fighter that her sisters were, but she wasn't anymore. She'd learned the hard way. It didn't pay to fight back.

Bitterly, she sat, quietly answering the doctor's pointed, specific questions, hands clasped tightly in her lap. Callie thought the inquisition would never end. Finally, forty-five minutes later, Dr. Lipinski released her.

"I'll take you home," Ty volunteered. With her right ankle injured, she wouldn't be able to drive her car.

"Good idea," Dr. Lipinski agreed. "I'm issuing you a pair of crutches for the next two weeks, Ms. Donovan. Commander, perhaps you'd be kind enough to go down to Supply, on the right, and pick them up for her?"

"Of course," Ty said, and he left with the chit authorizing the crutches.

Callie remained on the gurney, feeling very much alone in a way she had hoped never to experience again. Dr. Lipinski had given her a mild sedative to take tonight in case she couldn't sleep. Stuffing the pills into her purse, Callie squeezed her eyes shut in the silence of the now-deserted examination room. How could this have happened? It was her fault. Somehow, it must be her fault. Had she dressed too provocatively, bringing on Remington's unwanted attention?

Burying her face in her hands, Callie tried to get a grip on her roiling feelings. If Dr. Lipinski turned in that report, her career was as good as dead. She had no other training. There were no intelligence jobs in the civilian world. It was all she knew. Job security meant everything to Callie—much more than it did to her three sisters. They moved through life with a freedom that she envied. But then, her freedom had been taken from her long ago.

Feeling like a trapped animal, Callie slowly eased off the gurney. As torn up as she felt, she needed Ballard's company on the way home. A part of her wanted his continued support, even as another part— the part that distrusted men—wondered what his ulterior motives were. Ballard was a Top Gun—he was an instructor at the station. Someone like him didn't get that plum assignment unless he was the very best at what he did—aggressive, arrogant and selfish.

No, Ty Ballard was a pilot—and she'd be wise to remember it.

Chapter Three

"For whatever it's worth," Ty said as he drove the car off the station, the darkness surrounding them, "I'm sorry about what Remington and those two other pilots did to you."

Callie sat tensely in Ballard's car. She'd been silent since leaving the dispensary. Wearily now she said, "You don't need to apologize. It's not your fault."

His mouth barely pulled into a one-cornered smile. "In a way, it is."

Callie stared at his rugged profile for a moment. There seemed to be a vulnerability about him, although it was carefully closeted, and that appealed to her.

"What do you mean?" she asked.

"Well, before I got married, I caroused around a lot, too. I spent plenty of weekends drunk at the O Club, chasing the groupies." Ty shrugged and avoided her wide, intelligent gaze. "I don't believe that you teased Remington into following you out into the parking lot. From what you said to the doc, he was upset about that newspaper article and taking it out on you."

His apology, his insight, startled Callie. "I can't believe any navy pilot has the guts to admit he might have been wrong in chasing groupies. Most of those girls are eighteen and nineteen years old and don't know what they're getting into. The navy pilots at the O Club own that turf, and they see them as little more than property to be squabbled over." Bitterness hardened her words. "You're a surprise, Commander. I've been in the navy since I was eighteen, and I've never heard a man display those feelings."

With a teasing smile, Ty said, "Hey, we're not all bastards, you know." He desperately wanted to make her smile, but she had such an abandoned look that he felt helpless. When she didn't respond to his comment, he sighed. "I...I guess I never really realized until just now that the pilots play rough with a woman—whether she's asking for it or not. It makes me feel guilty."

"Then I guess that's one good thing that will come out of this mess," she muttered, "if one navy pilot sees that his chasing, his harassment of women, is wrong." Misery settled around Callie. Ty Ballard piqued her interest, but the threat of losing her career kept intruding on her emotions.

"I can't argue with you," he said, feeling bad for Callie. Streetlights flooded the car with cyclical regularity as Ty guided his sports car into the La Mesa area, where Callie had told him her apartment was. Finally, he pulled into the parking lot and shut off the engine. Her two-story apartment building was covered in stucco, of Spanish design with a red tile roof. Several palms lined the small, well-groomed lawn in front of the building.

"Let me help you to your apartment," he offered, turning toward her.

"No, you've done enough, Commander. You've more than done your duty."

Ty accepted her mutinous and accusing look. As he opened the door to get out, he murmured, "You've got every right to be upset. Use me for target practice. But I'm helping you to your apartment, no arguments."

Frustrated, Callie felt on the verge of crying in earnest. She couldn't fight Ballard's continued perceptiveness and solicitude. Was it just an act for her benefit? She'd never met anyone like him—a man who had so much awareness of other people's feelings. Most navy pilots were so egocentric that they existed in a very lofty, private world—a pilot fraternity they viewed as a close-knit brotherhood. Even family came second. Callie knew that divorces were the norm for navy pilots, and they frequently married two, even three times.

As Ballard opened her car door, she pulled the crutches from the backseat and fumbled with them. He stood back patiently, allowing her the time she needed to maneuver herself and the crutches out of the car.

"I *hate* the idea of being on crutches," she said tightly as she lurched to her feet, favoring her right ankle. Placing the crutches beneath her armpits, she glanced over at Ty. There was such sympathetic understanding in his eyes that Callie momentarily froze.

Despite the heavy contrast offered by the streetlight, which seemed to carve his rugged looks with light and shadow, she not only saw but felt his compassion. Angrily, she shoved it away. He was merely another representative of all the problems she'd ever had with pilots over the years.

Ty stepped aside as Callie began hobbling toward her apartment. He smiled briefly as he shut the car door behind her. "I have a feeling you don't like any kind of help," he told her as he walked slowly at her side, her purse tucked under his left arm.

Jerking a look at him, Callie said, "Commander, at Annapolis I got the message loud and clear. There is no support for women. I learned that lesson in my plebe year. No, I don't lean on anyone. Not ever."

The anguish in her tone needled Ty. "I went through Annapolis, too, so I know what you're talking about. We had three women in our group, and they took a hell of a lot of harassment," he admitted. "Two of them dropped out. Only one made it the entire four years."

Callie swung her way awkwardly up the concrete sidewalk. Luckily, her apartment was on the ground floor. Ballard was a product of his environment, there was no doubt. And the fact he was a fellow ring-knocker didn't thrill her, either. If she were a man, she'd be part of the vaunted brotherhood, that clique of male Annapolis graduates. But because she was a woman, she was coldly excluded.

"Square pegs in round holes," she said, stopping at the door of her apartment. Taking her purse from Ballard, she finally located the set of keys.

"Women have it tough in the military," Ty agreed quietly as he watched her open the door. A soft light emanated from inside, and he saw that the apartment was filled with green plants and the pale, Southwestern colors of sandstone, pink and lavender. Wanting to do more to atone for what had happened to Callie, he opened his hands. "Can I help you in any way? Make a phone call for you? I think your sister would like to know how you are. Or maybe a friend who can help you tonight?"

Touched by his concern, Callie shook her head. She saw care burning in his eyes, and heard real emotion in his voice. Giving him an odd look, she said, "Commander, I think you're a dream of some kind."

Ty cocked his head. "A dream?"

Callie tried to smile but failed. "I've never seen a pilot be so sensitive. You've been wonderful, and I don't know how to thank you. I'll be fine now," she answered steadily, although she felt anything but fine.

The shadowed look in her eyes convinced Ty that she was lying. But maybe she didn't even know it herself. He shrugged. "Like I said, we're not all cold, callous bastards. I know a lot of pilots who are good men, have families and a decent home life. Not all of them spend the other half of their life at the O Club." And then he sighed. "Not that I'm one to talk." When he saw her tilt her chin and give him a perplexed look, Ty smiled a little, as if to brush off the deprecating comment about himself.

"Thanks for everything."

Ty moved forward and touched her shoulder before she turned to shut the door. "Look, let me leave my phone number with you—just in case."

"No... thanks." A flash of panic darted through Callie. Ballard *was* a figment of her imagination. She saw the disappointment in his eyes, but he stepped away and shrugged. Now she'd hurt his feelings, and that was the last thing she'd meant to do. Torn by the evening's events, she whispered, "You're one in a million. I can get along by myself, now. Thanks."

"What about your car?" Ty said, grasping for straws, for any reason to see Callie again under less-pressured circumstances. He'd sworn he wouldn't even consider getting involved with a woman for at least another year. But Callie's blend of femininity, vulnerability and quiet strength drew him.

"I'll have my sister Maggie help me."

"Oh..."

"Good night, Commander."

"Call me Ty?"

Callie hesitated. She heard the hope in his voice and saw the plea in his eyes. As much as she wanted to, the past overwhelmed her. The last nine years of hurt were just too much to overcome. "No...I'm sorry, I can't."

Ballard knew enough to back away. "I'll be seeing you, Lieutenant Donovan."

The urgent knock on Callie's apartment door startled her, and she glanced at the clock. It was nine p.m. She'd been home exactly an hour. Picking up the crutches she hobbled disgustedly to the door and opened it.

Maggie stood there tensely, wearing jeans and a pink blouse. Her hair, usually pinned up on her head, swung loose around her proud shoulders. "Callie? What *happened?*"

Callie moved aside to let her sister in, then shut the door. "A run-in with my boss," she muttered.

Maggie's eyes widened as she took in Callie's condition. "My God, you look awful!" Her voice grew hoarse with disbelief. "Remington did this to you?"

"Take it easy," Callie said wearily, maneuvering back toward the living room. "Don't fly off the handle, okay? Right now, I can't take any more drama than I've already been through. Sit down. I'll tell you everything."

Callie watched the anger mount in Maggie's narrowed eyes as she related the story. When she mentioned Ty Ballard's name, Maggie leaped to her feet.

"That's The Predator!"

"What?" Then Callie realized that Maggie was referring to Ballard's nickname as a pilot. A chill went through her as she saw her sister's face change markedly with shock.

"Ballard's known as 'The Predator.' Don't you know who he is?"

"No," Callie said, "I don't. Remember? I've only been at the station for a month. You've been here nearly three years, Maggie. Besides, I work in Intelligence, not over at the Top Gun facility like you. Obviously you know more about him."

Maggie began to pace—a habit of hers, because she had trouble remaining still for more than two minutes at a time. "The Predator *helped* you?"

"If it weren't for him, I don't know how far Remington and his goons would have gone," Callie whispered, her voice cracking at the memory. "He broke up the fight, got me to the dispensary and drove me home. Really, he was very sweet about it."

Maggie snorted and halted, jamming her hands on her narrow hips in a typical pilot gesture. "Ballard isn't what I'd call 'sweet.'"

"Well, he was to me. In fact—" Callie sighed, feeling exhausted "—he showed some real sensitivity. That floored me."

With a shake of her head, Maggie muttered, "I can't believe it. Ballard's been going through one hell of a messy divorce, and he's a growling, snarling dog over at the Top Gun facility. In the air, he's murder on his students. You do know he shot down two enemy fighters in Desert Storm?"

"No," Callie said wearily. "So he did me a good turn. He probably felt guilty that his brother pilots did this to me."

Clenching her fists, Maggie sat down again on a nearby chair. She reached out and touched Callie's bandaged hand. "I'm *glad* Dr. Lipinski has reported this, Callie. It's the right thing to do."

Callie glared at her. "Maggie, I'm beat right now, and I'm feeling rotten. Don't start giving me your spiel about women's rights. I'm tired of it. I'm tired of being on the firing line. I took a direct hit for you tonight with Remington. He was angry about the newspaper article and what you said."

Maggie nodded apologetically. "I am sorry about that, Callie. Of all of us, you're the least likely to crusade." She touched Callie's black hair. "Is there anything I can do for you? Would you like to stay with me? Wes is out on a United Parcel flight to Europe and won't be back for at least a week."

"No, thanks."

Maggie smiled slightly. "You'll lick your wounds by yourself?"

"Yes."

"Like always."

"Like always."

Maggie rose and straightened the long shirttails of her pink blouse. "Call me tomorrow and let me know what you're doing, okay? I can get you groceries and stuff like that, if you want."

Maggie, for all her fire and warriorlike assertiveness, was the soul of care, and Callie loved this part of her sister deeply. "I'll let you know. First things first. The doctor has given me five days off from work with this ankle, so I've got to call my section head and let him know I'm not going to work tomorrow."

Grimly, Maggie picked up her purse. "First thing I'm going to do tomorrow morning is get in Remington's face. Who does that bastard think he is? I hate him. I hate his kind. He's not going to get away with it, I promise you."

"Maggie," Callie begged, "please don't start a fracas! I've got to work with Remington. My job's in jeopardy as it is. Don't make more trouble for me."

Maggie shook her head. "Dammit, Callie, he had no *right* to do that to you."

Tears swam in Callie's eyes, and she self-consciously wiped them away. "Look, I need to take a bath and get some sleep. I'm totaled. Just let me handle this. I don't need my big sister going in with boxing gloves and decking my boss—whether he deserves it or not."

Leaning over, Maggie hugged her sister. "Okay," she whispered. "I'll ease off the throttles. Let me know if Legal is going to press charges against Remington and those other two jerks."

Groaning, Callie released Maggie and sat back. "I hope not! That would mean a board investigation—and the end of my career. Oh, Maggie, I'm so tired of fighting this male system. We're outsiders. We've always been. All I want is to be left alone to do my job. Is that so much to ask?''

Gently, Maggie smiled. "Callie, in some ways you're so naive. I've been out on the leading edge, showing that women can fly fighter planes just as well as men. I know how brutal it is emotionally to take it again and again.''

"Yes, but you've always been a fighter.''

"You were once, too, you know," Maggie said softly. "But now you aren't. I don't know why...."

Uneasy, Callie shrugged. "We grow up, Maggie. You were Don Quixote tilting at windmills. You still are.''

"Yes, but my insistence, my strength to stay and take it, is opening up Congress to the possibility of women in combat. At least, in the air war.''

"I'll let you know what happens. Thanks for coming over," Callie said, abruptly, desperately trying to bring the visit to an end.

Maggie hesitated, opened her mouth—then closed it. She looked around the quiet, neatly kept apartment. "Are you sure you don't want me to stay or something? You look really pale and alone.''

Alone was the right word. Callie shook her head. "No, I'll be fine. Really.''

The doorbell kept ringing and ringing. Groggily, Callie pulled out of the sleep she so desperately needed. Rubbing her eyes, she sat up stiffly. Sunlight peeked around the venetian blinds, telling her it was well past time to get up. Looking at the clock on the dresser opposite the bed, she saw it was 0700. Who was at her door?

Her white cotton nightgown was badly wrinkled, but she pulled her pale green silk robe over it and tied the sash, hoping she looked half presentable. Still mystified by who might be at her door, she reached for the crutches and made her way out to the hall.

When she opened the door, her breath escaped. Ty Ballard stood there in a freshly pressed flight uniform, his cap in hand. He gave her a sheepish smile and appeared almost shy.

"Hi. I—uh, thought I'd drop over and see how you were this morning," he said awkwardly. "You didn't look very good last night, and I was worried about you." He groaned inwardly as he felt heat sweeping up his neck into his face. The truth of the matter was he had slept restlessly all night, thinking about—actually, feeling a lot about—Callie Donovan. He'd tried fighting it, but had finally awakened at 0600 grumpy and groggy from tossing and turning.

"Well—"

"I know it's early—"

They both spoke at once, then broke off.

"No, it's okay. Really," Callie said. She saw the concern burning in his startlingly clear gray eyes. In the morning sunlight, Ty Ballard was ruggedly handsome in his own unique way. He stood straight and tall, his shoulders proudly thrown back, his face recently scraped free of the beard that had darkened his features last night. Callie saw a flush touch his cheeks and realized he was blushing. How long had it been since she'd seen a man blush?

Trying to still his nervousness, Ty said, "I'd give you a line, but I think you've had a gutful of those lately."

With a grimace, Callie said, "I hate lines. They're so shallow." Pilots were shallow. Well, maybe not all of them....

"Yeah, we're famous for them, aren't we? Look, I thought I might take you out to breakfast or something, if you felt like it." He was having one hell of a time not staring at her. The green silk robe lovingly outlined her body. Her hair was disheveled, her eyes slightly puffy from just waking up. Ty found himself wondering what it would be like to wake up with Callie at his side. The thought came out of left field, so startling that it left him momentarily speechless.

"Oh, no..." Callie's heart was fluttering beneath his burning, hungry inspection, and she suddenly found herself at a loss.

Risking everything, Ty took a step forward and opened his hand in a gesture of peace. "Well, then, I'm pretty mean with scrambled eggs. I cook bacon reasonably well. How about if I come in and fix you breakfast before I head to work?"

She gave him a strange, searching look. "Why are you doing this?"

Ty stood nakedly beneath her scrutiny. With a one-shouldered shrug, he muttered, "I don't know. Out of guilt, maybe. I know Remington. And I know his reputation. You've only been at Miramar a month, and this isn't exactly a good welcome to the station. Maybe I'm trying to apologize." Well, that was partly true, Ty told himself. If Callie Donovan ever found out that he was genuinely drawn to her, he was certain she'd slam the door in his face. He didn't blame her for disliking navy pilots, but dammit, he *liked* her; and despite the circumstances, he wanted a chance to get to know her.

"I—"

"I'll be quick about it," he pleaded. "Come on, let me fix you breakfast." He held his hands up. "No funny stuff, I promise."

Callie's defenses crumbled beneath his warm, cajoling look. If she believed the sincerity in his eyes and voice, she could allow him this privilege. "I feel kinda awkward about this, Commander."

"Call me Ty." He took another hopeful step forward. He wasn't going to barge past her, or force himself on her. There was a fine line he was walking, and right now it felt like a double-edged sword. Callie's huge blue eyes were touched with doubt and wariness. "How about it? My mother didn't raise me not to cook and clean. Want to take a chance with me?"

The words felt like they were being etched into Callie's heart. Take a chance. How many times had she done just that and gotten hurt? But there was such a boyish demeanor about Ballard that she finally managed a small laugh and stepped aside.

"I'll bet you charm snakes for a living, too, Commander," she grumbled.

Euphoric, Ty moved into the highly waxed foyer. He had the good grace not to gloat too obviously about his victory. "Can't we be on a first-name basis?"

With a shrug, Callie shut the door. "I guess so."

He walked with her toward the kitchen. "Callie's an unusual name."

"Yes, my full name is Calista, but it got shortened at a very early age. I've always been called Callie."

He smiled as they entered the sunlit kitchen. "It's not run-of-the-mill, but then, neither are you. The name suits you."

"I'm not so sure of that," Callie murmured as she moved away from Ballard. Just being close to him was intimidating. He made her pulse jag erratically, and she sensed that aura of power around him, that indestructible confidence. She felt his gaze on her back as she moved over to the stove and counter area. No doubt about it. He made her very nervous.

"I'm going to shower and get into something more appropriate," she told him.

"Fine, fine. I'll make myself at home in the kitchen. When you come back, I promise you'll have a breakfast you'll never forget."

Callie hesitated in the doorway. Ballard looked positively happy. He placed his cap on the counter and began humming softly. With a shake of her head, she wondered which one of them was crazy. Her, for letting him into her apartment, or him for walking back into her life when he certainly didn't have to?

Although her ankle was badly swollen and the color of a ripe, purple plum, Callie was able to take a hot, invigorating shower. In her bedroom, she dressed in a pair of light blue slacks and a pink short-sleeved blouse, then called the station. She told the man on duty at Intelligence that she had a sick chit authorizing five days of rest. If Commander Remington wanted any more information, he was to contact Dr. Lipinski.

Glad that she didn't have to go in and face Remington, Callie sat on the bed and rewrapped her ankle with the Ace bandage. She had washed her hair, and now she took a brush to the dark mass. Because her hair was short, just above regulation collar level, it fell quickly into place.

Hating the crutches, she made her way on bare feet back out to the kitchen, from which wonderful scents were originating. Hungrily, Callie inhaled the aroma of frying bacon. Automatically, as she entered the kitchen, her pulse began to bound a little. Ty Ballard had tied one of her aprons around his waist. His sleeves were rolled up to just below his elbows, and he stood happily stirring eggs in the skillet. As if sensing her presence, he lifted his head and turned to look at her.

"Smells great, doesn't it? Come on, have a seat. I've set the table." Ty quickly moved over to pull out a chair for her. Trying not to stare like a slavering wolf, he forced himself to pay attention to the scrambled eggs. Callie looked like the proverbial girl-next-door in her simple slacks and blouse. And he liked the fact that she went around barefoot. Despite being one of the elite academy ring-knockers, she possessed an intriguing innocence that he ached to explore.

Callie moved to the table, which had been set with her good china, pink linen napkins rolled neatly beside the plates. A cup of recently poured coffee and a small glass of orange juice awaited her. Everything was perfect. She sat down and set the crutches aside.

"I'm in shock," she said.

Ty twisted to look over his shoulder as he added cream cheese and bacon bits to the scrambled eggs. "Over what?"

"You. This." Callie waved to the table. "Everything is so neat—thoughtful, I guess...."

"Brother, you must have had some bad experiences with men," Ty teased as he whipped the scrambled eggs furiously. "Some of us are kitchen trained."

His heartrending smile shattered her tension, and Callie laughed lightly. "I guess I had that coming, didn't I?"

"I don't know," Ty said smoothly as he brought the skillet over and served half the scrambled eggs to her and half to himself. "Maybe you haven't run into very many thoughtful men of late." He put the skillet in the sink, ran water into it, then quickly brought over the just-popped-up toast. Untying the apron, he laid it on the drainboard, then sat down at her elbow and grinned. "A meal fit for a queen. Dig in, Callie. You need some color back in those cheeks of yours."

Nonplussed, Callie picked up the knife and buttered her toast. Ballard seemed like a happy little boy instead of a serious navy pilot. "I don't know what to make of you," she muttered between delicious bites of the scrambled eggs.

"Why?"

"You're different."

Shrugging, Ty launched into his meal with gusto. "My ex-wife said the same thing." She might as well know he had a failed marriage. If nothing else, he had learned to be honest and keep all his cards on the table when it came to relationships. He knew he didn't want to make the same mistakes twice. Especially not with Callie. Even as the thought passed through his head, Ty wondered what kind of crazy magic had come over him. From that first moment of seeing her helpless in the parking lot, something had sprung loose deep within him. What was it? Loneliness? God knew, he'd been like a lost wolf without a mate since the divorce.

It was impossible to ignore Ty's upbeat presence. Callie glanced over at him when he mentioned the divorce. "You're single now?" she asked pointedly. Once, she'd fallen in love with a pilot who'd said he was divorced. It had been a lie, but he had strung Callie along, getting what he wanted from her. When she'd discovered the lie, she'd confronted Mark. He'd laughed and shrugged it off as if it didn't matter—as if *she* didn't matter.

Ty held up his left hand to show the absence of a wedding ring. "Single."

"How long were you married?"

"Five years."

She pushed the eggs around on her plate. "That's a long time for a navy pilot. Most of them seem to get married and divorced in two years."

"Or less," Ty agreed. He saw the wariness in Callie's face again. There was a lot of unspoken pain there, too, and he surmised that she'd been burned by a pilot at some point. "I liked marriage," he went on. "I liked the idea of having a home."

"Do you have any children?"

He shook his head. "No...."

"Is your ex-wife a civilian?"

"Yeah. She lives in San Diego. She's a bright, intelligent woman."

Callie heard the hurt in his voice, although he tried to hide it with bravado. "You said she called you 'different,' too."

"Well," he sighed, "'different' wasn't used in a complimentary way, Callie."

Callie thrilled to hear her name slip from his lips. Trying to ignore the feelings it invoked, she found herself wanting to continue pursuing Ballard's past. Why? she asked herself. Callie had no answers, and it left her feeling terribly vulnerable.

"Five years is a long time to spend with someone. You must have meant a lot to each other," Callie hedged. She saw her comment strike Ballard with a direct hit. His smile slipped, and a shadow came across his eyes.

"Jackie wanted the divorce," he said quietly. "I didn't."

"Oh."

Ty felt Callie's interest. He hadn't meant to get into a discussion about his personal life—at least, not this morning. He'd wanted to come over, cheer Callie up a little and head to work. He frowned, pushing the last of the eggs onto his fork. There was pain from the past to deal with, now, too.

"I guess I wasn't around when she needed me," he began. "I was gone a lot. Most of the time I was out on carriers—I didn't get the land-based assignments I'd hoped for."

"That ruins a lot of marriages," Callie agreed soberly. She reached over, placing her hand on his arm for just a moment. "I'm sorry. You seem nicer than most of the navy pilots I've known. It's too bad it had to happen, Ty."

Ty rallied under her soft, hesitant touch and the use of his first name. It was a start, and for that he was grateful. "Yeah, well, as the saying goes, the road to Hell is paved with good intentions. Look, I gotta run. I'm due to teach a class at 0800 over at Fightertown."

He pushed the chair away and stood up. Before he left, he placed his dishes and silverware in the sink.

Callie blinked at the abruptness of Ty's departure. She sat back and watched a mask drop over his rugged features. Unable to take offense at his sudden retreat into silence, she felt deeply for him. Ty had really loved his wife. That was a new twist for her. Most navy pilots loved 'em and left 'em without so much as an "I'm sorry," in her experience.

"Thanks for coming by... for everything," she managed in a small voice. She wanted to apologize for raking up the painful coals of his past. His suffering was obvious.

"Thanks for letting me barge into your life," Ty said. He picked up his cap and settled it over his military-short hair. "I'll be seeing you around. Maybe I'll call you in a couple of days—see how you're recuperating?" He'd never wanted anyone to say yes as he did now. Callie's upturned features were bathed with a pink blush that made her blue eyes sparkle with life— and suddenly Ty realized that his presence *had* helped her a bit. He felt good about that. He was just sorry he couldn't hide his hurt over the divorce. He cursed himself for bringing it up in the first place.

"A phone call would be fine," Callie agreed quietly. She saw a fierce longing burning in his gray eyes as he stood so proudly before her. The aura of a navy pilot was enough to knock any woman off her feet, she thought dizzily. And Ty Ballard was a very special man. Very special.

"Great." He smiled and lifted his hand in farewell. "I'll see you later, Callie. If you need anything, just call me at the office." He pointed to her ankle. "With that injury, you aren't going to be able to get to the commissary to buy groceries. Sure you wouldn't like me to help in that department, now that I've proved myself in the kitchen?"

With a laugh, Callie shook her head. "No, thanks, Ty. Maggie is going to shop for me after she gets off work this evening."

"I'll be seeing you around," he promised thickly.

Chapter Four

"Ty, Captain Martin wants to see you," Jean Riva said.

His cup of coffee in hand, Ty halted in the passageway of the Top Gun facility. He had exactly fifteen minutes before he was scheduled to start class. As always, the facility buzzed with muted excitement. Still euphoric over the possibility that Callie might actually like him, he nodded and stepped toward his commanding officer's office.

A short, dark-haired woman with piercing brown eyes that missed nothing, Riva was a GS-12 in Civil Service and was Captain Martin's very able assistant and secretary. But right now she looked unhappy. Ty halted at her desk.

"What's up, Jean?"

"A lot," she muttered. Leaning over, she announced Ty's arrival to the CO.

"Send him in, Jean," the gravelly voice on the other end ordered.

She straightened and nodded. "Go right in, Commander."

"No hints?" Ty teased. The woman was a no-nonsense, strictly-by-the-book civil servant of the best kind. She was famous for her organizational ability, because it was she, more than anyone else, who kept the facility glued together and functioning properly.

"No hints, Commander," she announced brusquely and gave him a cardboard smile.

Ty never liked that smile when Jean chose to use it. It meant she was holding back a lot of feelings about something—and usually it meant bad news. Girding himself, he sighed and opened the door. Bob Martin was one of the youngest captains in the navy. He was a highly decorated Vietnam veteran—an ace with six kills to his credit—and was even more no-nonsense than his vaunted assistant.

Martin's head snapped in his direction as Ty closed the door behind him. "Come in, Ty." He gestured toward one of the two chairs in front of his large walnut desk. "Have a seat."

"Yes, sir," Ty murmured, sitting down and balancing the cup of coffee on his left thigh. He often thought that Martin looked snakelike—but in the most positive way. He could keep his narrow face absolutely devoid of expression, and he had coal black eyes that never seemed to blink. They just stared down the other party with such an intensity that Ty figured Martin could mesmerize them into immobility—much the way a cobra would hypnotize its prey.

Martin's black hair was peppered with strands of gray at the temples, and now he was wearing his summer white uniform, the four gold stripes on black boards positioned on each of his shoulders shouting his authority.

"I understand you were a witness to the assault on Lieutenant Calista Donovan?"

Ty felt as if a bomb had been dropped in Martin's office. He straightened unconsciously. His CO must have received Dr. Lipinski's report via the legal department, he realized. "Er...yes, sir."

"Tell me exactly what you saw and what happened," Martin demanded in a clipped tone.

"Yes, sir," Ty said, and he launched into a brief sketch of the incident. He watched Martin's thin, black brows dip lower and lower as he completed the report. The man's mouth was a flat line by the time he'd finished, his dark eyes flashing with anger.

Leaning back in his chair, Martin turned and looked out the window that viewed the revetment area where the jets used for training sat. "Commander, I was hoping against hope that Dr. Lipinski was embellishing this whole damn thing." He turned around and placed his hands on the desk. "Obviously, she wasn't."

"No, sir."

"You've recently returned from a two-week stint at the War College, where you took accelerated courses in the Uniform Code of Military Justice, right?" he barked out, so abruptly that Ty almost jumped.

The UCMJ, as it was known, was a huge, legal compendium of articles that applied to every phase of military organization. Ty nodded. "Yes, sir."

Picking up a file near his left hand, Martin opened it. "And you were number one in standing, out of fifty attending officers?"

Flushing a bit, Ty murmured, "Yes, sir."

"Do you realize that somehow, by some*one*, this incident involving Lieutenant Donovan has been leaked to the major newspapers in San Diego and Los Angeles, as well as to press organizations around the United States?"

Stunned, Ty sat frozen, his grip on the coffee cup tightening. "No, sir, I hadn't."

"Any idea who did it? Not that it matters any-more—the horse is out of the corral now."

"I have no idea, Captain." Ty began to sweat. Did Martin know that he had fraternized with Callie after the incident? He felt as if the walls had suddenly grown eyes and ears. The discussion was on shaky ground, and he didn't know what Martin wanted from him.

"Well, within the next couple of hours, our station is going to be inundated with media attention. After that newspaper article by the Donovan sisters, things were already explosive." With a shake of his head, Martin muttered, "We've got a real problem, Ty, and we've got to move quickly to institute damage con-trol, or the navy could end up looking very bad—not only to our own tax-paying public, but around the world."

"Yes, sir." Ty sweated a bit more. He no longer chafed over the fact that he was going to be late start-ing his class.

"Here's what I'm authorizing. I'm convening a board of inquiry regarding this matter. Each of the officers listed in Dr. Lipinski's report will be given counsel by a fellow officer. Obviously, I can't assign just any officer to Lieutenant Donovan, or the press will cry foul play from the outset." Martin jabbed his finger in Ty's direction. "I'm ordering you to become Lieutenant Donovan's counsel. I can hold up your credentials as the officer at Miramar who has the most familiarity with the UCMJ. If I do less than that, the press will tear us apart. I'm not going to have someone accuse us of giving Lieutenant Donovan less than the best we have for her defense. Not on my station, and not on my watch."

Openmouthed, Ty stared at his CO. Never in his wildest nightmares had he thought he'd become a counsel in a board inquiry. It was something any officer could be ordered to do, however, and he quickly realized that by having the UCMJ training, he'd made himself eligible.

"But, sir, I'm teaching two classes a day here at the facility. To become a counsel is going to require a lot of time and effort."

Martin stared at him. "This is a UCMJ, Article 133 problem, Commander. Conduct unbecoming an officer. In this case, potentially three officers. I don't have a choice. We've got to move quickly to convince the press and everyone else, specifically Congress, that we are putting teeth into this board of inquiry. I know you have a stacked schedule, but if necessary, I'll relieve you temporarily and pull in someone TAD, to take over while you conduct the investigation on behalf of Lieutenant Donovan."

"But...I'm a witness to this, too."

"There's nothing in the UCMJ that says a counsel can't be a witness. When it's your turn to testify, you'll do exactly that. This isn't a civil case out in the public, Commander. I already checked to make sure it was all right for you as counsel to testify."

Ty was reeling. "This board will determine whether or not Commander Remington and the other two pilots should be disciplined. Is that correct?"

"This board will determine who is guilty," Martin snapped. "You're the best man for this assignment, Ty, so I want you to teach your classes today. After that, come and tell me whether you can balance both responsibilities. If you can't, you're temporarily relieved of duty as an instructor at Top Gun until the board is completed."

"When will the board convene, Captain?"

"In one week. You've got seven days to get whatever evidence, witnesses and information you can to present on behalf of Lieutenant Donovan. The board will be made up of three officers from your peer group. I won't be one of them, since it happened under my command. I won't have the press crying foul on that, too. Rest assured, we will gather three men with unquestionable backgrounds."

Dizzied by the news, Ty nodded. "Yes, sir."

"You've got exactly five minutes until your class starts, Ty. I don't want you or Lieutenant Donovan to speak to anyone from the media—is that understood? I'm putting a gag order on Commander Remington and the counsels involved with their side of this incident, too. The media *must* go through channels or all hell will break loose, and I will not permit that. Is that understood?"

Standing, Ty came to attention. "Very clear, sir."

"Good. Dismissed."

Callie was preparing a salad for her lunch when the doorbell rang. She wiped her hands on a nearby towel and settled the crutches beneath her arms. Who was it now? All morning, her phone had been ringing off the hook. Somehow, the incident involving her and Remington had been leaked to the press. Shortly after Ty had left, she'd received a call from Public Affairs at the station, ordering her not to talk to the media. They'd told her that more information would be forthcoming.

Opening the door, she once again saw Ty Ballard, hat in hand—but this time he looked very unhappy. A pronounced frown creased his broad brow, and his mouth turned down.

"Ty..."

"Hi, Callie. May I come in?"

She saw the briefcase in his hand and felt tension radiating around him. Her heart pounded briefly and she moved to one side. "Sure, come in."

"Thanks," Ty muttered. He shut the door. Callie was looking much better. Color showed in her cheeks and her blue eyes were no longer so fearful. He saw redness in them, however, and wondered if she'd been crying. The thought needled him. "We have to talk."

"Talk?"

"Yes. Business, Callie. I wish it wasn't, but it is."

She gestured toward the kitchen. "I was just fixing myself a salad for lunch. Would you like some?"

"No...thanks. I grabbed a hamburger on the way over here."

"Okay, you can talk while I eat. How about a cup of coffee?" She couldn't understand the tension in Ty's posture, or his abruptness.

"Sure, a cup of coffee sounds good." A drink would be better right now, he thought balefully: a stiff belt of whiskey.

In the kitchen, Callie finished preparing her salad and placed the bowl on the table. Ty poured them coffee and sat down opposite her. She hobbled to the chair and placed her crutches against the wall.

"I didn't expect to see you so soon," she said, drizzling Italian dressing over the salad.

"I didn't, either," he admitted ruefully. Opening his briefcase, he drew out a sheaf of papers and then took a pen from his breast pocket. "Look, you need to know what's going down, Callie." He hoped she wouldn't be upset, but that was fooling himself. "Has anyone from Miramar contacted you about what's going on?"

"On?"

"Yes, due to the incident."

With a shrug, she chewed a bite of salad. "About a half hour after you left I got a call from the station ordering me to not to talk to anyone from the media. That's all. They told me someone had leaked the story to the press, and I wasn't to say anything."

Taking a deep breath, Ty nodded. "Here's what is officially happening," he began, and he told her about the board of inquiry to be convened in one week's time. Then he squared his shoulders. "Callie, Captain Martin has ordered me to become your counsel." He held his breath, trying to ferret out Callie's reaction. Of all things, Ty didn't want this position. He'd rather have been left out of the loop on this incident all together.

"You?" Callie set her fork down on the pale pink mat and clasped her hands.

"Yes. Captain Martin wanted to ensure you had someone who knows the UCMJ. Now, I'm not a lawyer, and I want you to understand that."

"Do I need a lawyer?" Callie's heart began to pound with dread.

"Technically, no," Ty hedged. "But you can get one, if you want. That's your prerogative."

"How would the board see it?"

With a shrug, Ty muttered, "I don't know."

Rubbing her brow, Callie realized she was no longer hungry. She pushed the salad aside. "If I get a lawyer, it could go against me," she said. "The board is comprised of three officers, right?"

"Yes, three of our superiors."

She stared at Ty. Just how good was he at this sort of thing? "What is your function in this?"

"Basically, I'm your counsel. It's my job to find witnesses, corroborate testimony and do whatever I feel is necessary to place you in a good light before the board."

"And there's a counsel for the accused?"

"Actually," Ty said with a grimace, "under the UCMJ, each officer is allowed his or her own counsel."

Callie's eyes widened. "That means three against one!"

"I know it doesn't sound good," Ty said.

"Is there cross-examination by counsel?"

"Yes."

"Great," Callie whispered. "So, once I take the stand, I'm going to have three different male officers questioning me."

Squirming, Ty nodded. "I know it seems unfair—"

"It is!"

"You need to understand that they can bring in witnesses, too. Or experts. This is going to be just like a civilian trial in some ways, and whatever the board decides is final."

She stared at him. "My career is over, then. There's no way, Ty, that a board of three older male officers is going to believe my side of the story. And even if they do, I'll never live it down. My name will be known throughout the navy—and it won't be nice."

"Look," Ty pleaded, opening his hands, "I know this sounds lopsided, but—"

"You bet it is! I'm the victim in this, Ty. And I'm going to have three pilots swearing that I started it, that I asked for it, and three counsels coming at me with their teeth bared." Callie tried to calm her breathing. She felt shaky inside. "Oh, God, I never realized it would come to this. Why did Dr. Lipinski have to send in that report? I was just as happy to let it die."

Grimly, Ty reached across the table and slipped his hand over her knotted one. "Listen to me, Callie— Remington and those two pilots shouldn't get away with what they did to you."

His hand was strong and firm, and for a moment Callie felt safe. But she quickly pulled out of his grasp, fearing that if she didn't, she would open her hand and grip his back, even harder. "You actually think three pilots sitting on that board are going to side with me? I thought I was an idealist, but you're worse. I'm a woman, Ty. I don't care how tight our case is, how well you cross-examine those three bastards who did this to me, or how many witnesses—if any—come forward on my behalf."

Ty sat back, feeling helpless at the sight of tears gathering in her hurt blue eyes. "I'll do my very best to defend you, Callie. To bring the truth to light."

Rubbing her face, Callie whispered, "I have to think about this, Ty. I need to talk to Maggie. Maybe I ought to get a civilian lawyer. I just don't know. I need time to sort this out...."

"Okay," he said, putting the sheaf of papers back into his leather briefcase. "But we don't have much time, Callie. Can you talk to Maggie today and call me by this evening with your decision?"

Miserably, she nodded and allowed her hands to drop into her lap. The burning flame in Ty's gray gaze made her realize that he genuinely was there for her. "How do you feel about this?" she asked suddenly. "Did you want the job of defending me?"

His conscience needling him, Ty shrugged. "In all honesty, no," he admitted. "I have a tight faculty schedule, and I'm loaded to the limit with responsibilities over there."

Callie held his shadowed gaze, sensing more than hearing his words. "Being my counsel could hurt your career, too. Have you thought of that?" she asked softly.

Shifting uncomfortably, Ty nodded. "Yeah, I thought about it."

"You'll be going up against the brotherhood—trying to tear apart exactly what they huddle together to defend. They'll see you as a traitor."

"Yes, they probably will." Callie's face was pale, her eyes luminous with tears. It tore deeply at Ty. A woman's tears could level him as nothing else could.

"And yet, you're willing to do this?" she asked shakily. Then, the light suddenly dawning, she added, "Or, were you ordered to take my case?"

"I was ordered to do it," Ty said in a low tone. "But that doesn't mean I wouldn't have done it, Callie."

She eyed him for a long time, the silence building thickly between them. "Maggie said your nickname is The Predator."

"That's right."

"She didn't have many kind things to say about you. She thought you were as bad as any other navy pilot when it comes to harassing women."

Smarting under her accusation, Ty felt his skin prickling with heat. "That may have been true when I was single, but I never messed around after I got married the way Remington has. And yes, I've been guilty of chasing groupies. I haven't denied that."

"So what's changed?"

He was beginning to see the Donovan intelligence at work. Maggie was just as bone-baring, in her way, as Callie was now being with him. But in all honesty, he couldn't blame her. Why would she want someone who was just like the rest of the pilots to defend her? He knew she was questioning his ability to somehow prejudice his counsel position against her.

"Marriage changed me," he answered abruptly, after more than a minute of silence.

"You're divorced now. Why should I think you won't revert back to the same old navy pilot you were before? Why should I believe that you have the ability to defend me *honestly* when you're as much of a ring-knocker as the men who are accused?"

Anger flickered through Ty. He felt her own fury, and he understood it. "I may be lousy husband material," he answered in a clipped tone, "but I'm not the kind of man to go around taking unfair advantage of women. I never have."

Callie drew in a ragged breath, getting a taste of Ty Ballard's anger. "You've chased groupies at the bar. You've played all the little-boy locker-room games with them. I won't believe you if you deny it, Commander Ballard."

He flinched inwardly. Callie was on the defensive; she'd reverted to his official title. That hurt more than anything. "I won't deny it, dammit! Who's on trial here, anyway?"

Gasping, Callie pushed back the chair and got awkwardly to her feet. "On trial? You are, Commander! Why should I trust you any more than I trust Remington and his gang? Why should I trust a board of three male officers?" She grabbed the crutches, breathing hard. "Why should I trust *any* of you? I don't want to be in this position! I didn't ask for this! I just wanted to be left alone, can't you understand that?" Her voice broke and she stood there, gripping the crutches hard. "I won't get a fair board hearing— we both know that. My career will be ruined, my name smeared forever. And you know the saddest thing of all, Commander? I didn't start this! I'm the one it happened to!"

"Take it easy," Ty rasped, standing. "I know you don't like what's happened. If I were in your shoes, I wouldn't, either, Callie."

"Lieutenant Donovan to you, Commander."

Tension stretched palpably between them, and Ty realized he'd better leave. "Talk to your sister," he said as he picked up his briefcase. "I've left my phone number. You can call me tonight after you've made your decision."

Bitterly, Callie moved aside. "You know where the door is, Commander."

Trying to wrestle with the hurt twisting its way through him, Ty turned toward the door. He hadn't wanted the meeting to end this way. The pain in Callie's face had dissolved his anger, leaving only numbness in its wake. She was right on all counts: she was the victim, yet she was the one whose career, name and entire being would be under attack.

"I'll see you later," he croaked.

Maggie sat grimly on the couch listening to Callie's story, her hands folded and tense in her lap.

"Who's been assigned as your counsel?" she demanded.

Callie took a deep breath and whispered, "Commander Ballard."

Maggie shot off the couch. "What? The Predator? Come on, you've got to be joking!"

"I'm not, Maggie."

Pacing, Maggie muttered, "The Predator! Listen, that guy has a reputation that has followed him from early days. He's a killer in the sky, but he's also a hunter on the ground." Maggie halted. "Ballard is as bad as Remington."

"He said he changed after he got married," Callie answered wearily.

Lifting her hands, Maggie said, "I think the whole damn station is out to railroad you, Callie. Someone leaked this to the press. Do you know how many phone calls I've gotten today, asking me about it? About you?"

Callie nodded. She felt so old and so tired. "I feel like I'm preparing for the Spanish Inquisition, if you want the truth. But what can I do?"

Maggie began to pace. "Ballard is a competitive bastard, I'll say that much for him. What about a civilian attorney?"

"I've thought about it. The worst is, no civilian is going to be familiar with the UCMJ or board procedures, which could hurt me in the long run. Ballard has a strong background in UCMJ training, Maggie."

"Yeah," she snorted, "but he's one of the 'boys,' too. He's a ring-knocker. I've seen the brotherhood at work—they cover their tracks, defend their own kind."

"I know...."

"Hell," Maggie said, sitting back down, "we saw the 'good ol' boy' system at work when we went through the academy."

"You don't need to tell me," Callie said. "I just feel helpless, Maggie. No matter what I do, I'm hamstrung. If I hire a civilian lawyer, he won't know the ropes of the military legal system. If I depend on Ballard, he could—even subconsciously—be prejudiced against me because it's his 'brothers' on the line."

Bitterly, Maggie said, "Yeah, isn't that the truth?"

"Beyond the rumors, what's Ballard like? You work with him."

"He's intense. He's good behind the stick."

"Maggie, as a person."

"Oh. Well, he's been here about two years. I've flown against him as an Aggressor pilot, and we're even for wins."

Her patience wearing thin, Callie gave her sister a pleading look. "Give me a readout on him as a human being, Maggie. I don't care about his flying abilities."

Having the good grace to blush, Maggie ran her long fingers through her hair. "Sorry, sis. I get carried away."

"That's okay."

"Ballard is introverted. He's quiet, but intense. He's a good teacher because he has the ability to shift gears, level with the men he's teaching and reach them."

"Have you seen him at the O Club?"

"Sure. Usually, if we've been flying, we'll go over for a beer afterward."

Callie took a deep breathe. "Have you seen him chase the groupies?"

Maggie shrugged. "He sits with his buddies and drinks—not usually more than a beer or two. Once I saw a groupie go over to his table and try to hustle him, but he wasn't interested."

"Maybe this divorce has dampened his enthusiasm," Callie said.

"Who knows? I met his wife, Jackie, a number of times. She's a sharp lady. She's a stockbroker, I think. I do know that after she filed divorce papers, Ballard took a nosedive that I think he's still in."

"What do you mean?"

"He's just . . . different. Quieter, I guess. More introspective."

"Was it a nasty divorce?"

"Not from the scuttle I heard. It was a friendly settlement."

"Is he still friends with his ex-wife?" Callie hoped so. If he'd stayed on good terms with Jackie, that would suggest he didn't have a lot of anger and bitterness that could come to light in the courtroom—to Callie's detriment.

"I don't really know." Maggie smiled a little. "I could find out, nose around for you."

"It's too late for that." Callie looked at her watch. It was already 1900. She would have to call Ballard soon with her decision.

"We've got women flight mechs on the line," Maggie said, "and there's a woman on the team that maintains his F-14. My flight chief, Chantal, is good friends with this other woman—I think her name is Ardella Hecht. Chantal would tell me if there was any harassment going down, and I've never heard anything. So he must treat Hecht all right."

"How about women at the facility?"

"There are plenty of yeoman over there," Maggie admitted. "Ballard's always a gentleman with them. I don't see him following the secretaries around, and I haven't heard him dropping the type of innuendos that I have from that slime, Remington."

"Maybe that's a good sign," Callie murmured.

Maggie frowned for a moment, thinking, then sighed. "I don't believe you have a choice in this, Callie," she said unhappily. "Ballard is it. Which isn't to say that his past reputation doesn't worry me. Before he got married, he was in a lot of bar fights and brawls. I mean, he still swaggers. He's got Macho Navy Pilot written all over him, and he wears it like a good friend."

"I feel like I've been thrown to the wolves, Maggie. No matter what I do, no matter what my good intentions, my name, my career, is down the tubes."

"I know it's scary," Maggie agreed. "I'd hate to have something like this happen to me. I'd hate to think of the repercussions it would have on my career." She gave Callie a warm look. "But I'm puzzled, Callie. Ever since you entered the academy, you've changed. When we were growing up together, you used to be just as much of a fighter as the rest of us."

"I know...."

"Somehow—" Maggie looked at her assessingly "—you're going to have to get that fighting spirit back."

"I don't want to fight anyone!" Callie cried. "I just want to be left alone."

Maggie came over and sat on the arm of the chair. She placed her arm around Callie. "I'm sorry, sis," she offered gently. "I'm afraid it's too late for that. But I'll help you any way I can. If Ballard wants me as a witness, I'll be there for you."

Sighing, Callie wrapped her arm around her sister's waist. "Right now, I can use all the support I can get."

"There's nothing I'd like better than to face off with that bastard, Remington."

Chuckling, Callie glanced up at Maggie's set and furious features. "You'd probably throw a punch and deck him right in front of the board."

Laughing, Maggie hugged her and stood up. "Naw, I wouldn't do that. I'd just take Remington apart, piece by piece...."

The moment of laughter passed, and Callie watched her sister pick up her purse to go. "I'm really afraid, Maggie. My career is everything. I don't have any other skills if they kick me out."

"They can't kick you out," Maggie said.

"You know they can pressure me into resigning. I've seen other people pushed out of the navy for various reasons. They can do it to me, too."

Her eyes glittering, Maggie said, "Not without one hell of a fight, Callie. And that's what you've got to do—you've got to learn to fight back. Ballard's a fighter. I know he's not perfect, and his past is suspect, but at least he'll wade into that ring with boxing gloves on. You'll have to do the same."

"*If* Ballard can really side with me, and believe in me," Callie said. "He was ordered to take the case, Maggie. So what does that say?"

"Ballard's reputation with the groupies may be shot, but I'll give him this—he's got a bit of the knight on a charger in him, too. He's very clear about right and wrong."

"Great. But what if he thinks I asked for Remington's attack? Then he won't side with me."

Reaching down, Maggie squeezed Callie's hand. "Talk with him. Get him to come over and sit down, face to face, and spill your fears. Gauge how he reacts to them, Callie. Then, if you still feel he'll betray you, go to Captain Martin and demand another counsel. That's your right."

"This is such a mess."

"No denying that, sis. Look, give Ballard a chance. Call me after you've made your decision, okay?"

Her heart heavy, Callie nodded. "Okay. And thanks, Maggie..."

"Donovans always stick together," Maggie reminded her grimly. "And just remember, you're out on the leading edge for all women. This little incident is a lot larger than you realize. The newspapers know it, that's for sure. Right now, you're a symbol for women, whether they're civilians or in the service."

"I don't want to be a symbol," Callie said bitterly. "That's your bag, Maggie. You wear it well, and you've done wonders for women who want to fly fighters in the navy. But I don't want that responsibility. I'm not the fighter you are."

"You," Maggie said softly, "don't have a choice. Let's make the best of this—for all women."

Chapter Five

Callie jumped inwardly when her doorbell rang an hour and a half later. It was Ty Ballard, she knew. When she'd called him shortly after Maggie left, he'd answered the phone with a growl, obviously still upset from their last brutal meeting.

Emotionally girding herself, she answered the door and stepped aside. It was dark, the warm, dry California air filtering in and mixing with her apartment's air-conditioning as the door swung wide. Ty Ballard stood before her, grim-faced, his briefcase in hand. But this time, instead of a uniform, he was wearing civilian clothes.

Callie swallowed convulsively, drawn powerfully to his shadowed features, the late-day darkness of beard lending his face a dangerous look. Ty wore a dark red short-sleeve shirt and beige chinos. His white tennis shoes seemed inconsistent with his fighter-pilot and military-officer image.

"Please," Callie whispered, "come in." The phone call between them had been terse and monosyllabic. She hadn't wanted to discuss the agenda over the phone, wanting instead to judge Ty's facial reactions as they talked.

"The kitchen?" he demanded in a brusque voice.

"Yes."

Ty moved through the foyer, heading directly to the kitchen. He still smarted under Callie's distrust of him, but he was trying to get a handle on his anger. He knew it wasn't her fault.

Hearing her coming, he looked up from the briefcase he'd set on the table and opened. In the light, Callie looked more washed out, more defeated, than ever before. The edge on his anger melted.

"Would you like some coffee?" Callie asked.

"No, but I could use a drink at this point. Some whiskey, if you've got it."

Cringing beneath his blistering look, Callie knew she had to stand strong and be counted. She didn't want to wilt the way she usually did under the withering fire her fellow officers sometimes aimed at her. Or she would use her favorite defense and run and hide. But this time she couldn't do either. Maggie was right: she had to reach down into the wellspring of her soul and somewhere find some courage—and fast.

"I don't have hard liquor. Will wine do?"

"Yes." Ty snapped his briefcase shut and set it down on the tile floor with a little more force than he intended, the sound echoing through the kitchen. Callie had limped to the refrigerator and drew out an unopened bottle of wine.

She took the wine to the counter and searched in a drawer for the corkscrew. Ballard's unhappy presence was enough to make her hands shake as she popped the cork on the green bottle. She turned and saw him sitting at the table, looking like a bullterrier ready to bite her. Could she blame him? She'd accused him of many things, some of them unfairly.

Moistening her lips, she placed the bottle on the table with two crystal goblets. "You pour," she instructed as she sat down opposite him.

Ty said nothing, but he tipped the bottle as she'd directed. The tension was electric. He didn't know what to expect next. Callie, despite her paleness, had a resolve he'd never seen before. He felt it, too—a kind of invisible strength that enveloped her. Handing her a glass filled with the pinkish blush wine, he got up, retrieved the cork and put the wine back in the refrigerator for her.

Running her fingers slowly up and down the slender stem of the goblet, Callie waited until Ballard had sat down again. He lifted his glass.

"To us, whether either of us likes it or not."

She stared at him, the cynical words grating on her feelings. "Hell of a toast, isn't it?" she asked candidly.

"We're in a hell of a situation," he shot back.

"You said 'we.'"

"Well? Isn't that correct?"

Callie held his cold, gray stare and matched it with one of her own. "I'm not apologizing for anything I said earlier."

"I didn't ask you to."

"Men expect women to cower or back down in the face of confrontation."

"Let's get one thing straight, Lieutenant Donovan—you're not the normal 'woman' and I'm not the normal 'man.' Can we at least agree on that?"

"There is nothing normal about our situation. That I will agree on, Commander Ballard." Callie held her glass steady as she barely touched it to the lip of Ballard's glass, never breaking eye contact. She'd had practice at this as a kid, she thought incongruously, when she and her sisters would try to stare one another down—to see who could go longest without blinking.

"You're one tough lady when it's time to get in the trenches, do you know that?" Ty acknowledged, giving her a grudging score against him. He sipped the cold, sweet wine. This was a new and fascinating side to Callie Donovan—her strength was showing through. Surprised but pleased, he took a second gulp of the wine to soothe his frayed feelings.

"How do you think I survived the academy, Commander?"

"Touché." Ty took a third and then a fourth sip of the wine. He set the glass aside and folded his hands in front of him. "Okay, are we on for this board thing?"

"Yes."

"You've thought about getting a civilian attorney?"

"Yes, and it isn't feasible. He won't know the UCMJ as thoroughly as you do."

Pleased at her analysis, Ty gave a bare nod of his head. "Okay, that passes the first hurdle. What about me?"

"My sister filled me in on you."

His brows moved up a fraction. "Maggie?"

"Yes."

"What did she say?"

"That's private, Commander. What you need to know is that I feel I can trust you—at least up to a certain point—with being my counsel."

"Where don't you trust me?" Ty clamped down on his slow-burning anger. Callie had stirred up a lot of old, painful memories from his destroyed marriage.

"Where?" Callie smiled grimly. "You're a man. You're a ring-knocker. The men who are going before that board are ring-knockers, too. The brotherhood sticks together against all comers, Commander. And I know I'm seen as a threat to you and them."

"Hold it," Ty growled, raising his hand. "Don't you think you're a little arrogant to be lumping me with Remington and his kind?"

"No, because before you were married, you may have been as bad as Remington."

Easing back in the chair, Ty held her challenging gaze. "You're accusing me of not trying to give you a fair chance at that board, then."

"I guess I am. But I don't have a choice, Commander Ballard. And I can't really blame you. I think the peer pressure of the brotherhood, which is heavily weighted in numbers at this station, will be brought to bear on you if you do try your best to win my case."

Holding on to his building fury, Ty glared at her. "Where do you get off accusing me of that kind of stuff? You don't know me. You know nothing about my morals or values."

"Commander, I know the academy. Remember? They mold you. They play with your head. They mess with you until you break and do things their way. Four years of brainwashing does wonders. I've been in the navy for nine years and I've repeatedly watched the brotherhood close ranks on me and other women officers whenever their position, their authority or potential rank, was threatened by one of us." She tapped the table with her finger. "The glass ceiling is well in place in the navy. I'm just letting you know that I'm going into the hearing with my eyes wide open. I don't expect anything from you, Commander."

Anger and hurt soared through him. Ty caught himself and realized that it was because he liked Callie Donovan so much that her assessment of him cut so deeply. Wrestling with that realization, and fighting to salvage some kind of relationship with her, Ty put a steel grip on his escalating fury. "You expect me to betray you?"

"Yes," she continued calmly. "Whether you mean to consciously or not, I believe the peer pressure will force you to not do your best—to not investigate this matter to its fullest extent."

Ty's eyes rounded. The charges seared him. He shoved the chair away from the table, the legs grating loudly against the white tile floor. "You are really paranoid, lady."

Callie watched him move to the counter, turn and face her fully, anger clearly etched in his eyes. "That's right, Commander," she answered, refusing to back down. "I know the system. I've been screwed by it again and again—only this time will be worse. Because I'm a woman, I'm a second-class citizen in the military—an outsider. Don't worry, I'm cognizant of the psychological reason for why it's this way in the navy, and I grudgingly accept them—whether I like it or not." Callie took a deep breath and willed herself to keep her gaze focused on Ballard, although her heart was pounding. "Do you know why I accept it?"

"I'd like to," he conceded.

"Because I love my job," she answered simply. "I love what I do, and I believe in serving my country the best I can. If that means working with one hand tied behind my back, being cheated out of earned promotions by a male officer who has less on the ball than I do, then so be it."

Clenching his teeth, Ty realized her attack on him wasn't personal. It was aimed at the entire male-dominated system. The anger sloughed away, and he stood there for a long moment assimilating her honest appraisal of the military. Finally, opening his hands, he offered, "Yeah, it's rough on a woman."

"Life is rough on a woman, Commander, but I'm not going to get into that. I live in a microcosm called the navy. Well, my number is up and there's no escaping it now, as much as I might want to. From what Maggie says, I don't believe you'll deliberately sabotage my case, but I do feel you'll bow to the pressures that will without a doubt be brought to bear on you."

In spite of himself, Ty almost smiled. There was a toughness to Callie that he liked one hell of a lot. More women needed this kind of inner strength but didn't have it—or perhaps they suppressed that possibility within themselves, he realized. His ex-wife certainly had it. And he'd screwed up by not recognizing or supporting that facet of Jackie. Instead of reveling in her natural strengths he'd been threatened by them, and had tried to break her. By the time he'd realized what he was doing, it was too late. In his need to dominate Jackie, their love had been destroyed. The lesson had been a harsh one. And Ty had sworn never to forget it.

Studying Callie, her black hair neat and soft, her lips set, her eyes narrowed with fear and determination, Ty silently promised her that he wouldn't fail her as he had Jackie.

Working his mouth, trying hard to hold his emotions at bay, Ty muttered, "I know my reputation around here is a little jaded."

"That's putting it mildly."

His slight smile was bleak. "My ex-wife is a very strong woman, Callie," he began, deliberately using her name to try to reestablish a more friendly, teamlike rapport. "In fact, she's a lot like your sister Maggie. I made some serious mistakes. Instead of respecting Jackie's strengths, I tried to control her and them, thinking that she shouldn't be like me."

"You mean, that she shouldn't be like a man in some ways?"

"Yes, she was very assertive—a go-getter."

"Men praise a fighter pilot for being aggressive, but if a woman pilot has the same moxy, she's seen as pushy," Callie offered.

Ty nodded as he came back over and sat down. "That's how I saw my ex-wife. She accused me of setting a double standard, and I admit now, I did." He shook his head, feeling old pain. "I caused the destruction of the marriage because I wouldn't respect her in those areas. By the time I realized what I had done, it was too late. Too much water had gone under the bridge, I'd said too many damaging things. I wanted to try to make up, to get back together, but she said no."

Callie not only heard, but felt Ballard's pain. What had it cost him to admit this to her? She knew how arrogant, how cool and icy fighter pilots were—and how out of touch with genuine emotions they could be. Seeing the regret in his gray eyes, now dark with anguish, she lost some of her edginess toward him.

"Well," she murmured, "maybe I've been a little harsh in accusing you of not trying to win my case for me."

"Maybe not," Ty said. "I hamstrung Jackie in a lot of ways. I've had a year to reflect on what I'd been doing to her, the emotional games I played to try to keep her in her place—or what I thought was her place."

She gave him a strange look. "And what did you learn out of that?"

The question was incisive and Ty silently praised Callie for her insight. "I learned that you can't categorize women. I used to have this image in my head—and yes, maybe it was shaped by the academy—about women. I've been seeing them in a different light since my divorce, trying to realize it's okay if they're as assertive as men."

Callie gripped the glass on the table in front of her, intuitively evaluating Ballard's honesty. He looked lost, in one respect, as if the discovery of allowing a woman to be herself had taken its toll on him. Sipping at the wine, she held his gaze. "And since your divorce, have you gone back to your old ways, Commander? You know, reputations die hard in the navy."

Ty grimaced. "I do go over to the O Club after work—especially after flying a Mach 3 for a couple of hours—to get a beer. But that's it. I don't hang out with the guys anymore, and I don't hang out with the groupies.''

Should she believe him? His words fit with what Maggie had told her she'd seen.

"So what do you do with all that time on your hands, Commander, if you haven't gone back to your watering hole?" Callie couldn't help the slight derision in her tone. Four years of brainwashing at the academy had taught her just how effective the brotherhood was against a woman officer. Could Ballard really have slipped out of that mode?

Ty finished off his wine and set the glass aside. "Since my divorce, I've more or less buried myself in work. After my time is up here, I want to be a test pilot at Patuxent River in Maryland. In order to do that, I've got to get up to speed on aeronautical engineering. I'm working on a second degree right now, so a lot of my time is tied up in night school."

A little more relief sped through her. "I see...."

Ty leaned forward, his hands clasped in front of him. "I know the navy isn't perfect, Callie. I know I'm not, either, but your career, to put it bluntly, is on the line. You and I both know that, although the board will deny it." He drew a paper from the sheaf at his elbow. "The board has brought sexual harassment charges against the three pilots under Article 133 of the UCMJ, conduct unbecoming an officer."

"Sexual harassment," Callie repeated dumbly. "Not assault?"

Ty saw the anger in Callie's narrowed blue eyes. "The CO of the station read Dr. Lipinski's report and evaluated it that way."

"But I was pushed and shoved. I was slammed against the car and to the ground. Doesn't that con-

stitute assault?'' Her voice cracked with anger and she
reared back in the chair. "Oh, brother, I can see the
handwriting on the wall on this one without ever going before the board. They've already lessened the
charges so that the pilots won't get what they deserve.
The brotherhood is working, isn't it?''

"Hold it, Callie. You weren't exactly forthcoming
and descriptive to Dr. Lipinski about what happened
to you, either. She can't read your mind. She had to
pull every stitch of information out of you."

Callie sat angrily for a moment, breathing hard, her
chest hurting. "Because I knew it would hurt my career! I'm trapped!"

"Surviving is tough," Ty agreed quietly, trying to
soothe her. She was angry, but her eyes told him of the
pain she carried for the many injustices she'd endured
during her years in the navy. "The navy has a zero-
tolerance policy toward sexual harassment."

"Sure," Callie grated. "Look the other way and
pretend it didn't happen—that's how zero tolerance
works in the navy."

"I won't argue that point with you," Ty said. Just
the way the light moved across her sleek cap of hair,
picking up bluish highlights, made him wonder what
it would be like to stroke those silky strands. That was
hardly a professional thought, he chastised himself
immediately. But there was something terribly vulnerable about Callie that aroused an unexpected
yearning in some buried part of him.

Wearily, Callie pointed to the paper in his hand.
"So, it's sexual harassment charges?"

"Yes."

She felt as if she'd already lost the case. "What
happens next?"

Ty placed the paper aside. "Most of it happens on my end. I've got a week to prepare our side."

"Among your other demands of school and teaching?"

"I'm asking my boss to relieve me of my teaching at the Top Gun facility so I can give this my full attention."

Callie's lips parted in disbelief. The officer corps at Top Gun thrived on getting their daily or weekly F-14 flights and playing fighter pilot, she knew—often at the expense of everything else in their lives. For Ty Ballard to walk away from his first love in order to take on her case said something startling about him. Maybe the divorce really had opened his eyes to the fact that women had every right to be themselves. Swallowing, Callie said, "I never thought you'd do something like that."

The softening in Callie's eyes made Ty feel like a soaring eagle. Instead of her usual wariness, he saw respect glimmering in her gaze, and it made him happy in a way he'd never experienced. "I just got back from a two-week course on UCMJ reporting procedures," he admitted a little shyly. "One of the areas that was covered was sexual harassment. There's a defined way of going about collecting background information for such a case."

Callie sat back in her chair, dazed. "I feel a little lucky, for once."

Ty smiled as the hope surfaced in her voice. It was all crazy, he decided, this chance encounter of meeting Callie. But in his heart he knew that there was something good, something worth exploring with her, and he wasn't going to give up on her—or it. "We got off to a bad start," he continued smoothly, "but I'm not letting that stop me with the investigation I have to do."

How badly Callie wanted to believe that Ty was one hundred percent in her corner. But the old, ingrained experiences of the past hammered at her newly found hope, reviving her sadness. Despite all that, she liked him on a personal level, she had to admit to herself. How many men could be as open as he'd already been with her? "I want you to be brutally honest about this with me, Commander. What is the best I can hope for out of this board?"

"Can we be on a first-name basis?" Ty asked. "Frankly, for something like this, formality isn't going to cut it. I need you to realize we're a team, Callie. I'm not some ogre out to get you. And I'm not going to knowingly sandbag your case because I happen to be a ring-knocker." He opened his hands toward her. "How about it? Can you trust me?"

A lot of feelings thrummed through Callie as she sat digesting his plea. Her gaze ruthlessly delved into his, searching his face. Her ears keyed in on the tone of his voice for a long moment before she answered. "I want to trust you," she began haltingly, "but I can't. Not really." With a wave of her hand, she added, "The past is in the way, and I hope you can realize that I've had some bad experiences that make me distrustful. I *can* call you by your first name, if you want." With a shrug, Callie knew she couldn't apologize, nor should she, for how she felt. Still, a large part of her, the part that liked Ty, felt terrible. Above all, Callie knew she had to be honest—even if it hurt both of them.

A part of Ty responded to her soft tone, and he felt her anguish, no matter how she tried to hide it. What had happened in the past to make her so distrustful?

He wanted to ask, wanted to pursue that avenue, but realized it wouldn't be beneficial right now.

"Okay," he said in a low voice, "you're being honest, and as much as I don't like to hear it, I appreciate it."

"A part of me does trust you, Ty."

Hope rose in him, then was tempered. The corners of his mouth drew in to a deprecating smile. "But a larger part of you doesn't?"

"I guess," Callie admitted wearily. It was late, and she was exhausted by the day's roller coaster events. "Normally, I run and hide. I don't like confrontation. I...just don't."

"In this case," Ty said, as he gathered up his papers, "let me do the confronting for you. I happen to think you've got a good, basic case against Remington and the others. What he did to you was unconscionable. Unforgivable. I don't care what he tries to tell the board, I intend to shred him and his defense."

Callie lifted her head and heard the steely confidence in Ty's lowered voice. She saw anger in his eyes and realized it wasn't aimed at her—it was aimed at Remington. A little more of her battered hope surfaced. Did she dare trust that Ty Ballard was willing to attack the brotherhood in her defense? No, her head whispered, he'd never forsake his pilot brothers for a woman, no matter how clear the evidence. Yet the stern look on his rugged features made her believe differently. Maybe it was her damning idealism that rallied within her. But idealism had gotten her into so much trouble in the past. And idealism without a link to reality was dangerous. How well she knew that.

"I want you to get a good night's sleep," Ty told her as he rose and replaced the papers in his briefcase.

"I'll do a little reconnoitering tomorrow morning, find out who will represent the three accused, and then come over here around 1000. We're going to have to write a thorough report of what happened. I want you to try to remember the exact words used by each of the pilots—what you said, they said, what each player did."

Ty snapped the briefcase shut and stood there, his long hands draped over it. Callie Donovan was nothing like her sister Maggie, he realized. In comparison, Callie behaved like a beaten animal, cowed and wary. His heart opened to her, and Ty felt a tug at his emotions that he hadn't experienced in this long, cold year since his divorce. And although Callie appeared wan, he also could register the hope, the caution—and the underlying strength-in her eyes.

What he would have to do was play upon and support her strength and belief in herself—help her feel confident that she had a right to be heard and vindicated before that board. Callie didn't really believe he could do that for her, and Ty felt a little like a knight whose armor was badly dented, rusted along with his reputation. In the past he had been as bad as many of the pilots, that was true. He'd been a woman-chaser, and he'd done it purely for the challenge of netting and taming the women for his own selfish needs and desires.

A lot of water had gone under that bridge, he realized belatedly as he stared down at Callie. Jackie had taught him much about women and their capacities. He now could respect women, not needing to lump them into "safe" stereotypes. Further, because of what had happened to Callie, he was only beginning to realize how much those old behaviors victimized women, and he felt old guilt. But could he convince Callie of the change within? If she couldn't completely trust him, then the board hearing would not work in her favor. She had to trust him fully, as if her life depended upon him—which, in some ways, it did.

Yes, he had to gain Callie's trust. But how? He only had seven days. Ty felt as if he were facing a double-edged sword. To gain her confidence, he had to establish intimacy with her on some level. But in doing that, Callie might misinterpret his behavior. Right now, what he really wanted to do was put the briefcase aside, walk over, take her in his arms and hold her. Simply hold her. But she might see his way of comforting her as something completely different— and that would smash the trust factor completely. Ty felt trapped and uncertain.

"I'll see you at 1000," Callie said, rising to her feet. She could see a longing, some unnamed desire banked in his gray eyes, and an ache flowed through her, strong and sharp. Caught off guard by the rush of feelings, Callie held out her hand. "Thank you, Ty," she whispered.

Just the shining hope in Callie's eyes made him feel like living again. Ty thought he saw something else in her expression, but it was fleeting, and he couldn't interpret it. Could it be interest in him as a man? He fervently hoped so. He smiled a little and grasped her smaller hand. "Don't thank me yet. We've got a long road to climb—together."

His hand was warm, dry and firm. For an instant, Callie wanted to throw herself into his arms. Just to be held. Just to feel safe for a moment. The tenor of Ty's deep voice, the feel of his hand encircling hers, told her that he'd offer that to her, if she wanted. She saw the mixture of need and respect in his eyes. The clash of her own yearnings forced her to pull her hand from his.

"I don't know about this 'together' thing," she said uncertain. "I've been so alone so long, fighting my own battles, that I don't know if I can be a team member in that sense, Ty."

Her gut-wrenching honesty touched him as nothing else could. Ty stood there, only a foot away from her, and began to realize what the navy had done to Callie. Admiration for her, for the fact that she loved her job and was patriotic to her country despite all the prejudice she'd experienced, rose in him.

It was useless. Without thinking, Ty reached out to touch her cheek. He caught himself and drew his hand back. The look, the surprise in Callie's eyes told him much: he saw no accusation in her gaze, rather a softening, as if she would have welcomed his touch. Would she? Terribly unsure, he allowed his hand to drop to his side and gave her a reluctant smile filled with apology. "Let's take it one day at a time, shall we?"

Callie felt suddenly breathless at the look she'd seen in Ty's face—the outright hunger for her in his expression. Startled but overjoyed that her sense about him wasn't wrong, she took precious moments to regroup her scattered emotions. There *was* something intangible, something beautiful and clean, that existed between them after all. The discovery was bittersweet. Callie intuitively felt that Ty had reached out to touch her cheek because he saw she needed care—desperately. But was this her idealism coming out again? She couldn't be sure. With a nod, Callie agreed. "That's good strategy."

Ty wanted to reach out again, to cup her flushed cheek and give her some kind of reassurance. The need was intense, and it caught at his breathing. Forcing himself to move—knowing that if he didn't, he was going to do the wrong thing—he eased around Callie.

"Just have a pot of coffee on, okay?"

Callie watched him hesitate at the entrance. Her mouth drew into a sad smile. "Sure." She saw him lift his hand, then turn and disappear. After the door closed, Callie felt suddenly bereft. Abandoned. With a shake of her head, she realized that Ty Ballard's overwhelming male confidence and presence had made her feel a little safety for the first time in her nine years in the navy. That in itself was an amazing discovery.

What would the morning bring? Callie's heart fluttered in nervous response to that question as she hobbled out of the kitchen and made her way to the large, roomy bathroom. A part of her was thrilled at the idea of seeing Ty again; another part wasn't. The war between her head and her battered heart continued as she drew herself a bath. Sprinkling orange-scented crystals into the clear water, Callie undressed.

As she sat on the stool and unwrapped her swollen, black-and-blue ankle, she laughed suddenly. That's how she felt emotionally: bruised. But the feeling was nothing new. It had been in place since the academy. Now her physical body was merely mirroring how she felt inwardly.

She glanced at the Ace bandage that she used to keep her ankle supported and in less pain. Could Ty become that for her on an emotional level? With a shake of her head, Callie moved carefully into the tub of fragrant water. She was becoming idealistic again.

In her romantic life, she'd known only navy officers. All had been pilots. And all had abandoned her
in some way. Ty Ballard would be no different, she
reminded herself with heartbreaking clarity. He
couldn't be. Leopards didn't change their spots—not
ever.

Chapter Six

Ty arrived promptly at 1000, wearing his summer white uniform. Somehow, Callie thought, although heaven knew she'd seen thousands of men in uniform, Ballard was impressive. He wore his garrison cap, its patent leather bill black and shiny. His white uniform and hat gleamed in dark contrast to his darkly tanned skin, the jacket's shoulder boards emphasizing how broad his shoulders really were. Most of all, he exuded a confidence she wished she had.

This morning, Callie noted, his face was freshly shaven, the dark growth that had shadowed it the night before gone. It made him look less intense, but his gray, alert eyes held that same look, and made her feel a bit more hopeful than she had since she'd awakened. Offering him a hint of a smile, she gestured for him to come in.

Ty nodded and took off his cap and placed it beneath his arm as he entered the foyer. Callie looked positively beautiful in such a refreshing way, he thought. Her black hair was recently washed, still damp and clinging to her head, the tendrils curling slightly at her temples. She'd paired a turquoise oversize shirt, its sleeves rolled up to her elbows, with a pair of white cotton slacks. And she was barefoot!

Ty managed to keep to himself the smile that wanted to creep across his mouth. The many facets of Callie Donovan were as surprising as they were stimulating. He liked it that this navy-academy officer was willing to go barefoot. He liked her style, and he liked her ability to stay true to herself despite her background.

Callie's cheeks were flushed, emphasizing the blueness of her expressive eyes, as did the shirt she wore—and a dainty pair of turquoise-and-silver earrings. If possible, Ty thought as he walked down the hall to the kitchen, Callie looked a little more relaxed. He took her barefoot state to be a sign of some trust. His spirits lifted unaccountably, and he felt like whistling, his habit when he was happy.

He hadn't whistled in over a year, Ty realized as he set his briefcase on the table and waited for Callie to appear on her crutches. He smiled suddenly. Callie might see herself as a quiet shadow who worked in the background, unseen and unnoticed; but the woman had an incredible effect on him!

Callie came around the corner and saw Ballard smiling. His entire face became less harsh, less intense, and in that startling moment, as she stood poised at the entrance, she saw a very human, very vulnerable side of him. The discovery jammed in her throat, momentarily suspending her breathing.

"Oh, there you are," Ty said, realizing that Callie was stopped in the doorway, staring at him, her lips parted, her eyes filled with something like shock. "Come on in," he murmured, quickly swallowing his smile beneath a more businesslike aspect.

Afraid to ask why he'd been smiling, Callie said nothing. She'd already set the coffee cups on the table. Now she went to the counter to get the steaming, fragrant liquid to pour into them. Feeling almost giddy, she struggled to keep a closed expression on her face as she poured the coffee.

"Thanks," Ty said, as he pulled out the other chair for her. He flushed as she turned and came toward him. "I want to tell you how pretty you look, but I'm afraid you'll take it the wrong way, under the circumstances."

Touched by his admission, Callie's lips softened. "Thank you for the compliment, and you're right—I could take it the wrong way right now." She sat down and watched him move around the table to take his seat. His short-sleeved white shirt and his white slacks were impeccably pressed and starched, accenting not only his dark tan but the thick black hair covering his arms. Ballard was such an intense, masculine kind of man that Callie felt slightly off balance around him. He appeared not to realize his effect on her, and she wondered if it was a sham, or if he really didn't know his charisma was so overwhelming.

Sipping the coffee, Ty realized appreciatively that gentle classical music was playing in the background. Sunlight lanced through the lacy curtains at the large windows above the kitchen sink. On the window shelf at least six small, potted plants were lined up. The different odors in the kitchen, which seemed to be coming from the plants, were alluring.

"Are those cooking herbs?" he asked.

"Yes."

"Are you a gourmet cook?" he teased her.

Callie tried to settle her pulse and appear business-like. "Upon occasion."

"Nothing makes me happier than a good meal," he murmured.

"Oh, that old adage of a woman getting to a man's heart via his stomach?"

"Ouch, no, I didn't mean it that way." Ty was beginning to realize how touchy Callie had become. He couldn't blame her, but it was going to put a definite damper on the normal off-the-cuff remarks he usually shared with his friends.

"I thought you were suggesting I invite you over for dinner some night," Callie stated bluntly.

Ty's eyes twinkled. "Well, I can't say the thought didn't cross my mind—and stomach," he admitted, "but I'm not going to put you in the position of having to turn me down, given what's happened."

Callie tilted her head. "What do you mean?"

Ty stopped spreading out the papers necessary for the report. She seemed genuinely stymied by his admission. "After being harassed by three navy pilots, I don't imagine you want another one in your life—for anything except professional reasons. If I were you, I'd be feeling pretty down on navy pilots. I wouldn't want them anywhere around me."

"That's a projection," Callie said.

"No," Ty hedged, "I'm trying to put myself in your shoes. I've been trying to do that all morning. What would I feel like if this had happened to me?"

"You're surprising me," Callie admitted with a shake of her head.

"Oh?"

"I've never met a navy pilot who thought of anyone but himself." She knew that was harsh. Surely there were some nice guys out there—she'd just not had the good luck to meet them. Until now, perhaps....

"I think," Ty said lightly, trying to help her relax, "that we men have got that coming. You're right—most pilots are not only filled with a lot of self-confidence, they're also self-centered."

"My heart be still," Callie laughed, placing her hand against her breast. "I never thought I'd live to see the day a navy pilot would say that about himself, much less his brothers."

With a grin, Ty felt joy flood him at the sound of Callie's husky laughter. The light in her eyes was like the sun-gold flecks against the deep blue of her gaze. Her lips were soft and curved, and he suddenly ached to know what it would be like to touch them with his mouth, to explore her, and tap into that fire he knew burned hot beneath her cool exterior.

"Believe me when I tell you that my divorce was a great leveler. It pointed out my shortcomings very succinctly." He lost his smile and picked up a pen. "I hope I've learned from it. I hope I never see women the same way."

"You're something else, Commander. This is the first time in nine years I've seen a man in the navy come clean with the truth."

"Ordinarily, I wouldn't share this with anyone," Ty said, now serious, "but I've got to do something to make you realize you can trust me, Callie." And never had he wanted a woman to trust him more. Last night, too, he'd slept restlessly, tossing with thoughts and feelings, all centered on Callie.

"There's that word again."

"I know." With a sigh, he gestured to the forms spread in front of her. "My counsel will only be as good as the information you supply me with." He held her earnest gaze. "That means you have to trust me with your deepest, darkest secrets—that you have to come clean, too, in a sense. I just found out that Remington has hired a civilian attorney to represent him—an ex-navy captain who worked in Legal."

"Oh, no!" Callie felt her heart begin to thud slowly. That meant that Remington was going to fight back with every bit of power he could muster and afford. "He's worried about this affecting his career," she said bitterly.

"Obviously." Ty saw her face fall, the bleakness returning to her eyes. "Don't blow this out of proportion, Callie."

"Don't?" She sighed. "Why shouldn't I? This legal eagle is a full-fledged attorney. He's ex-navy, and I'll bet he's a ring-knocker, too."

"His name is Jason Lewis, and yes, he's an Annapolis graduate."

"I knew it!" She sat there breathing unevenly for a long moment, and tried to gather her strewn emotions. "And he's a retired captain. He's probably got more rank than the board that's convening." She looked up at Ty for verification and saw him barely nod.

"The board has three commanders on it," he elaborated. "Two men and a woman. As you know, it must be comprised of your peers. You're a lieutenant, so that meant either lieutenant commanders or commanders."

"Lewis is a captain. I don't care if he's retired or not, the board will respect that. They'll take it into consideration, Ty!"

Wincing at the desperation he saw mirrored in her eyes and voice, he said, "They shouldn't take it into consideration."

With a snort, Callie rasped, "They will! It's a good-ol'-boys' club. I'm the outsider. What a joke. I'm the one who was attacked, but that doesn't even play into this comedy of errors. And I'll lay you anything that this Lewis will come after me like a wild dog ready to rip my throat out."

"Not if I can help it."

"How does a board work?" she demanded tightly. "Do I get cross-examined? Does the board ask me questions? What kind of cross fire am I going to be in?"

It was a war of sorts, Ty thought, but he didn't want Callie to know that—at least, not yet. "I'll ask you questions, and then the counsel for each pilot will have the opportunity to cross-examine you," he admitted. "The board may also ask questions whenever it chooses to. Only one person takes the stand at a time. The rest remain in the room, but are quiet. Take it easy," he pleaded. "There's no sense in getting overemotional now. You're going to have to take all these feelings and mold them into some very clear thinking when we go into that board session."

"Take it easy? Ty, my career is as good as gone!"

He leaned forward, his voice low with feeling. "If that's the way you see it, then we have to fight to get it back, don't we?"

Callie closed her eyes and tried to contain her roiling anger at the unfairness of the situation. Somehow, just the fact that Ty said 'we' made her feel a little better. Opening her eyes, she gave him a stormy look. "Let's not fool ourselves about what's going to happen. My career is dead in the water. They'll somehow make it out to be my fault. I just know it."

"Not if I have anything to do with it," Ty stated grimly.

"Remington and those two other pilots deserve to be kicked out of the navy, as far as I'm concerned, Ty. But the board will probably slap their hands, say, 'Bad boys!' and let them walk away scot-free. In the meantime, it will be my career that's damaged, because I came forward to protest what they did to me. It isn't fair! It just isn't!"

When the tears formed in her eyes, Ty couldn't take it anymore. Searching for and finding the white linen handkerchief in his back pocket, he held it out to her. "Don't cry," he mumbled. "I can't stand to see a woman cry. It tears the hell out of me."

Callie glared at him as she dabbed her eyes and blew her nose. "Well, how do you think all of this makes me feel? You come in here and tell me Remington has hired this big legal gun with all the right breeding, the right credentials. He's out to smear me and ruin my career."

Ty couldn't argue with her. He wasn't a lawyer. He wasn't a captain, either—just a mere lieutenant commander. And worst of all, he didn't have the expertise that Lewis did in the field of law. "Okay," he snapped, "so we're underdogs. That shouldn't be new to you, should it? Being a woman in the navy, you should be used to that position in the hierarchy." Dammit, he wasn't going to accept Callie's victimlike perspective.

Her head snapped up, her mouth dropped open and her eyes widened at his challenge. "Why, you—"

"Cut it out, Callie. I'm not here to give up on your case. I don't care if the world's most famous attorney shows up at that board—it doesn't matter to me." He tapped the report in front of him. "What does matter is the truth."

"Even if I'm right," she cried angrily, "that doesn't guarantee I'll win this board hearing. It doesn't even guarantee that I'll have a job when it's all over! That's what you don't want to comprehend. The truth has nothing to do with this, don't you see that?"

"No," he snarled, "I don't see that. I'll never see that, dammit! I happen to believe in the system, and yes, it's flawed, but I know it can work. If I can't believe in that, then I shouldn't be in this navy."

Wiping her eyes jerkily with the handkerchief, Callie glared at him. "What an idealist you are, Commander. Well, let me tell you something from my view of the navy as a woman officer, there will be continued unfairness toward me. I'll be seen as the troublemaker, the one who started this whole mess. It's okay for a man to have a gripe, but if a woman does, she's considered mouthy. And it's okay for a man to stand firm on what he believes, but if a woman does the same, she's 'hard' or 'tough.' And if one of these pilots loses his temper, it shows how much he cares about his work. If I lose my temper for the same reasons, I'm bitchy."

Callie gulped back a sob. "You see, there are two sets of laws, two legal systems out there. One is visible, but the one that really works is invisible."

"I think you're paranoid," he rattled defensively.

She gave him a cutting smile. "We'll see, won't we? I've been through the system too many times. You're the one who's going into this like some knight galloping toward the charge on your white horse. And you're the one who's going to get the surprise. I'm prepared for it. I'm prepared to be seen as the perpetrator, the tease. I'm prepared to have my career destroyed and to be given my walking papers."

"That won't happen!"

Sadly, Callie shook her head. "You're a very good human being as far as pilots go, Ty, but you don't get it. You can't, I guess, because you're not a woman. I'm telling you," she whispered as she handed back the handkerchief to him, "that we'll lose this board hearing, that Remington and those other two pilots will walk away without any just punishment."

Ty sat back and refolded the handkerchief, damp with Callie's tears of frustration and anger. "I just don't know how you could say those things," he muttered, putting the handkerchief back into his pocket. "I believe in the navy system. I believe in their zero-tolerance policy. I've seen it work. No, I don't care how much you want to give up on your case, Callie, I won't let it happen. And if you want to see me as some knight charging a dragon that's going to devour both of us, that's fine, too. But I don't see myself that way. I see that we have a case—an open-and-shut sexual harassment case that is winnable. I expect to nail Remington and those two other pilots. I'm going to ask for the maximum punishment for Remington, and

I'm going to ask that the other two pilots have their careers shaped by what they've done."

Wearily, Callie sat back, her arms folded over her breasts. The light burning in Ty's gray eyes told her of his sincerity to fight on her behalf. Why couldn't he realize that he could never win for her? "By the time you're done trying to defend me, you'll understand," she whispered, her voice cracking. "You'll see what the navy really thinks of the women who serve."

"I don't believe it. I never will."

Callie pulled a notebook from the desk near the table where the phone sat. "Do you know how many phone calls I've received from other navy women since my case hit the newspapers yesterday?" She opened it and showed him a list of eight names, phone numbers and addresses. "At least twenty women, about half of them enlisted, the other half officers, have called me."

Ty glanced at the list and then looked at Callie. "What did they call for? To give you support?"

She laughed, but the sound was mixed with sorrow and outrage. "Ty, these women called to tell me *their* stories of how they'd been sexually harassed. They called to wish me well. They called to tell me that they hadn't had the courage to report the victimizers because they were afraid."

"Afraid?"

"Yes, for their careers, for the retribution they knew would be heaped on them." She shook her head. "And I've got to tell you, one of the women was more than harassed, she was brutally raped—by her supervisor, so she's really afraid to come forward." She looked down at herself. "What happened to me wasn't so bad after all. But I never realized that until these women called."

Sourly, Ty sat watching Callie's face. "Because I took you to the dispensary, you didn't have a choice about reporting it or not."

"I know. That's what I told them. I told them I was really a coward at heart—that I hadn't wanted it reported for the very same reasons they didn't come forward. I didn't want a board investigation. I didn't want any of this."

Ty looked at the names in mild shock. He'd never realized the insidiousness of sexual harassment until now. "Yes, but Remington and those two are going to think long and hard before they ever attack another woman because you have come forward." He tapped the paper. "Have any of these women been sexually harassed by Remington or those other two pilots?"

"I don't know. They didn't mention names, they're so scared of being found out. Why?"

"I'm going to talk to them."

"No!" Callie came out of the chair, her hands resting flatly on the table. "No, you can't do that. They called me in confidence. They don't want to be found out. Please don't do that, Ty. Don't."

He couldn't stand the look of devastation on Callie's features, so he nodded. "Okay."

"You mean that?"

"Sure. Why wouldn't I?"

Taking the notebook that held the names, she closed it and placed it under the telephone directory. "I—I don't know."

His mouth compressing, Ty scowled. "You think I'd sneak around behind your back, don't you?"

Biting her lower lip, Callie slowly sat down. She'd hurt him; she could see it in the shadows of his gray gaze. "I...well, yes. I'm sorry, you didn't have that coming. You've been more than fair with me. And highly tolerant. I know I'm bouncing around like a yo-yo emotionally.''

Without thinking, she reached out and touched his hand. The black hair on the back of it was thick and wiry. She felt the instant tension of his muscles, the inherent strength within him. When she saw his gray eyes soften and lose their hardness, her throat constricted. "I'll bet you're sorry you were out there that night in the parking lot,'' she whispered. Hesitantly, she withdrew her hand. Just that brief contact with Ty had banished some of her instability.

Stunned that Callie had reached out and touched him, Ty sat there for a moment assimilating the gesture. Her touch had been tentative, feather light. Swallowing hard, he held her sad gaze. "Just the opposite,'' he rasped thickly. Risking everything, he captured her hand in his. Surprise registered instantly in her eyes. "I have to admit, my life has been turned inside out. But I'm not sorry, Callie. I never will be.'' Tightening his fingers around hers, he said in a low voice, "More importantly, you have to trust me.''

For a moment, Callie allowed herself to capitulate, to believe that she could trust Ty. The burning look in his eyes spoke of his passionate commitment to defending her. His hand was warm and strong. Caring. It was foreign to her to be on the receiving end of that kind of caring from a man. She'd seen it between Maggie and her husband, Wes, so many times—that sense of thoughtfulness, of being more concerned with the other than themselves.

Bowing her head, Callie closed her eyes, her voice strained. "I've been really hurt in the past by men, Ty. I know I'm making you pay for others' behavior when

I distrust you. You haven't done anything to earn that from me, but I just can't seem to help how I feel.''

"It's okay," he said quietly, giving her hand one final squeeze before he forced himself to release it. If he didn't, he was going to lift her hand, kiss the back of it and ruin what little trust he'd just established with Callie. When she raised her head, her eyes were bright with unshed tears. For a moment, he wondered how someone as emotional and sensitive as she was could possibly survive, even thrive, in such a harsh male climate where she knew she wasn't welcome. It spoke of Callie's underlying strength, Ty knew.

"Listen," he said, clearing his throat, "we need to get back on track. I'm going to lead you through this board procedure one step at a time. There are certain things I need to touch base with you on, requirements in preparation for a board investigation."

Nodding jerkily, Callie forced herself to pay attention to the business at hand—and not remain focused on Ty Ballard. Her hand tingled pleasantly where Ty had held it. There was such latent strength in his grip. "Okay." She picked up the coffee mug and took a drink.

Shaken by the intensity of their contact, Ty scowled and took a paper, turning it around for her to view. He wanted to say to hell with the formalities, put this trial aside and simply get to know Callie, the woman. But that was impossible, so he quietly closed that part of his heart and hoped for another chance at some point in the future. "I need to give you a definition of sexual harassment so that you will understand where and how I'm going to focus the investigation."

Leaning forward and trying to concentrate on the paper, Callie nodded, the cup of coffee between her hands. "I know what sexual harassment is—nearly every woman does—but tell me the working legal definition of it," she said wryly.

"Basically, it's inappropriate or illegal behavior by one person toward another. Usually, it's committed by a man toward a woman, but sometimes—maybe five percent of the time—it's reversed."

"And the other 95 percent of the time harassment is committed by men," Callie drawled. "Why am I not surprised?"

"Save your anger for the hearing," he warned her with a slight smile. "The definition can include negative or offensive comments, jokes or suggestions about fellow employee's gender or sexuality."

"Remington and his gang certainly qualify on that one."

"You'll get your chance to try to recall exactly what they each said in order to corroborate that fact," Ty said. "It can mean obscene or lewd remarks or jokes, or calling you things like 'sweetie,' 'honey' or other more inflammatory nicknames."

"Like 'split tail.' "

Ty jerked his head up. *Split tail* was a highly derogatory term sometimes used by men in the navy toward navy women. "Who called you that?" he ground out.

"Remington. Who else?"

Anger coursed through Ty, and he snapped his mouth shut against a curse he wanted to level at the officer. Forcing himself to get back to the matter at hand, he said, "It also includes talking about or calling attention to your body or your sexual characteristics. If Remington has bothered you at work and you've objected to his 'attention,' that's also included in the definition. It's also sexual harassment if nude or sexual pictures, photographs, cartoons or calendars are displayed on navy property."

Callie sat back. "I didn't realize all of this was included in the definition."

"We're not only going after Remington for his harassment and attack on you a few nights ago, we're nailing him for anything he might have done to you over at the Intelligence unit."

Releasing a sigh, Callie rolled her eyes. "Ever since I got here, he's been trying to grope me."

Ty held up his hand. "Let's start at the beginning." He picked up the report. Taking a tape recorder, he pressed the Record button. "This little machine is in case I omit something from the report that ought to be in there," he told her.

Callie's paranoia doubled at the thought of her words being recorded. In the wrong hands, it could kill her career. But she stopped herself. If Ty Ballard was putting on a front, it was completely fooling her. She vividly recalled his hand gripping hers and him pleading with her to trust him. Did she have a choice? Swallowing, she avoided looking at the tape recorder sitting off to one side of the table.

"Okay, the beginning," she said unsteadily. "The first day I reported in for work, I had to go to Remington's office. He got up, shut the door, came up behind me and slid his arm around my shoulders. He told me I'd be the prettiest navy officer working under him." She scowled. "Believe me, he put emphasis on the word *under.* As a matter of fact, he leaned over and whispered it in my ear."

Frowning, Ty forced himself to write down the incident. "What was your reaction?"

Callie laughed abruptly. "I was in shock. I'd never had any boss do something that blatant."

"But you have been harassed by other bosses?"

"Sure. Maybe a look. Maybe a vague innuendo that left me wondering if I had somehow invited that kind of response."

"That's the other problem with harassment victims," Ty said. "They often think it's their fault. They look at the way they're dressed, if their skirt is too short, if they're wearing too much makeup or whatever."

"As you well know, navy regulations keep our skirts knee length." Callie sighed. "And as for makeup, I never wear any, although I've been asked by various bosses to do so."

"That's harassment of another kind."

"Looking back on it, I suppose it was. I just shrugged my shoulders and told them I preferred the natural look."

Ty smiled slightly and glanced at Callie. "You look beautiful without any makeup. Stay that way." And then he caught himself and laughed. "That wasn't a sexual-harassment comment, either."

"Why wouldn't it be?" Callie asked, curious and thrilled by his compliment.

"First of all, whatever is said has to be taken by the woman as inappropriate or in some way illegal or disrespectful. Did you take my comment as any of those?"

Callie flushed and looked away from his dancing eyes. "No, of course not."

"Well, there, you see? Now, maybe if I said something like, 'Not only do you look good without makeup, you'd look good in nothing at all,' that would be sexual harassment. There aren't many women who would find that complimentary."

"Just the opposite. I find it offensive and suggestive."

"Bingo. You're catching on fast, Callie." He smiled fully.

"By taking my deposition, are you going to try to hang Remington for *all* that he's done to me?"

Ty shook his head. "No, I can't do that, because you never officially reported what he's done to you over at Intelligence. But what I can do is paint a picture for the board to show that Remington has a past history of this kind of behavior toward you. It can't be entered as evidence, but can be considered surrounding or background information."

Callie's esteem of Ty rose another notch. Even if he wasn't a lawyer, he was thinking like one, and that made her feel a tiny bit better about her chances. "What else do you have planned?"

"I need from you the name or names of anyone who was at the O Club that night who might have seen you."

"Remington came over to the dining room where I was eating and started hitting on me, then," she recalled grimly. Snapping her fingers, she sat up. "I know! Lieutenant Andy Clark was there. He was only two tables away and I know he heard the whole embarrassing conversation." Callie touched her cheeks, which had gone hot at the memory. "I felt like crawling under the table. I felt like dying."

Ty felt her anguish and humiliation. Glumly, he wrote down the name and tried to hold on to his anger toward Remington. "Great, we've got a witness."

She became sober. "You really think so, Ty? That guy is a fighter pilot, too. He's also a ring-knocker. What makes you think he's going to break the silence and defend me when he's sworn to protect the brotherhood?"

With a shrug, Ty murmured, "Look at me. I'm an academy graduate, and I'm on your side. Who's to say a second pilot won't do the same thing?"

Callie had grave doubts, but somehow Ty's ebullience in the face of such seemingly insurmountable odds gave her hope—and something more. As she sat in the kitchen, watching him write furiously in precise, painfully neat script on those forms, she was struck by him as a person. Not as a fighter pilot, not as an officer in the navy, but as a man.

Perhaps she was so gun-shy, so injured by harsh experiences with navy pilots that they had clouded her view of Ty Ballard completely. He was warm and personable and seemed to be the soul of sincerity, she saw now. The look of anger in his eyes as she told him what Remington had done couldn't be faked. Nor could the quavering tone of fury in his deep voice. Touching her brow, Callie took a deep, shaky breath.

Her world had been turned upside down. And her job was on the line. She would have felt much less secure, much more panicky if Ty Ballard weren't sitting across from her. It was him, she realized. Ty had a rock-solid sense about him, and it transferred to her. All hell was breaking loose around her, but Ty had become the eye of the hurricane. Now, if she could only give him her trust, that would be a fair exchange. If only...

Chapter Seven

"How's it going, sis?" Maggie—dressed in a pink tank top, white shorts and her favorite, very worn tennis shoes—stepped into the foyer of Callie's apartment and gave her a measuring look.

"Okay, I guess. Come on in. How was work today?"

Maggie grinned and walked slowly with Callie to the living room. "Same as always—exciting."

"I don't know which you love more, Wes or that F-14 you fly."

"They're both lovers, only in a different sort of way," Maggie answered with a laugh. "Wes is number one, however, in my life."

"Whew, that was close!" And Callie joined Maggie's lilting laughter.

Flopping down on the overstuffed lavender couch, Maggie tossed her purse aside and pushed off her tennis shoes. She brought her long legs up and folded them beneath her. "How did it go with Commander Ballard this morning?"

Callie lowered herself into a pale blue chair and lay her crutches on the carpeted floor next to her. "This morning? We didn't get done with the report until late this afternoon."

"Really?"

"He's thorough, Maggie. And a lot smarter than I gave him credit for."

"Both are in your favor." Maggie smiled a little as she assessed Callie. "Are you still so distrustful of his intentions in taking on your case?"

"No...not as much," she conceded. "He's sincere. Still, he doesn't realize what it's like to be a woman in the navy."

"And the harassment of different sorts we put up with to do a job we love," Maggie added grimly.

Callie sighed. "I think he's starting to get the larger picture, though. Since the article came out in the newspaper yesterday, I've gotten over twenty calls from other navy women, both enlisted and officer, who had been harassed."

Maggie's brows shot up. "Are you serious?"

"Never more. What's heartbreaking is that some of the women have had a lot worse done to them than what happened to me."

Sitting up, her feet on the floor now, Maggie clasped her long, thin hands between her thighs. "Did you tell Ballard about that?"

"Yes. He wanted their names so he could talk to them, but I told him no. These women want to stay anonymous because they're afraid of being punished by their male superiors, or of losing their job."

"You could lose yours," Maggie warned.

"I know, and I'm scared to death. I mean, what else am I trained for? Who wants an intel officer who can read satellite and photo recon maps?"

"There's no great call for it in the civilian world," Maggie agreed glumly. "Now that Ballard knows the whole story, does he think you've got a chance of being cleared by the board?"

Callie told her sister everything, and by the time she was done, Maggie was agitated.

"Remington's a slick bastard," she muttered defiantly. "I never liked him—he's such an arrogant jerk. He thinks he's irresistible to any woman."

Shivering, Callie said, "When he touched me that first time, I felt nauseated. His touch is so slimy. Every time he looks at me, I feel as if he's undressing me."

"I just wish he'd tried that on me."

Callie smiled a little. "You'd deck him. Maybe I should have."

"Then he'd have *you* up on assault charges. No, but you could have told him to get his slimy arm off you and never touch you again."

"He's the type that would have taken my rebuff as a challenge, Maggie. Then he'd have dogged my heels more than he has already."

"I'm looking forward to being here for the hearing," Maggie said, changing the subject. "I called Ballard this morning before he came over here, and told him that if he needed me as a witness, I'd be more than happy to go before the board in your behalf."

Touched, Callie said, "You could be hurting your career by doing that, Maggie."

With a snort, her sister rose to her feet and put on her tennis shoes. "It's time women learned to stand together and fight. If we don't, these guys will keep singling us out, destroying us, and then going on to the next woman victim. No, we've got to start banding together and defending one another in any way possible."

"I think it's already beginning to happen," Callie said. "The women who called me all asked if there was anything they could do to help me—short of testifying. I was really touched, Maggie, by their outpouring. Several of them are coming over—a sort of group meeting. They wanted to meet and talk with other women who've had similar experiences. If nothing else, I think it will be good group therapy for us."

"That's wonderful," Maggie said. "Your standing up and saying, 'I'm mad as hell and I'm not taking it anymore,' may give them the courage to come forward, too." She picked up her purse and walked over to Callie. "I just wish Remington had tried this on me and not you."

Callie reached out and squeezed Maggie's offered hand. "Your career means just as much to you as mine does to me."

"I can always get a job in the civilian world pushing passenger planes around in the sky," Maggie chuckled. Becoming serious, she squeezed Callie's hand in turn. "I'll drop over and see you tomorrow night before I go home."

"Isn't Wes due back tomorrow?" Callie knew that as a pilot for the worldwide conglomerate of United Parcel Service, he was frequently gone a week at a time, hauling cargo from one country to another.

"Yes, but he'll understand. See you later, sis."

Ty couldn't contain his need to see Callie the next afternoon. He'd worked all morning at his office, gathering evidence, making phone calls and piecing together vital information for her case. Now he stood quietly, waiting for Callie to answer her door. Inwardly, he wasn't still at all. Last night he'd dreamed about her—soft, lush, torrid dreams. Since the divorce, he'd shied away from women. Callie was re-awakening him to his desires. But the feelings went beyond sexual. There was some intangible, magical gift that she gave him simply by being herself. And more than anything, Ty wanted permission to continue to explore this new and exciting experience—something he'd never encountered with any woman before Callie had unexpectedly fallen into his life.

Right now, he wasn't sure how she felt toward him—or if there was a shred of hope that she might be interested in him as he was in her. They were caught in a cross fire, brought together reluctantly. And he knew Callie didn't trust him to bring her safely through the storm that threatened her and her career. But Ty wasn't going to let her down. The divorce had given him new awareness and insights—about women in general, and about himself as a human being. Armed with that hard-earned knowledge, Ty was determined to make this work between them.

Laughing at himself—at his longings that only days ago he'd thought had died, never to return—he waited impatiently for the door to open. When it did, he couldn't help but smile down at Callie. Today she was dressed in a bright, flowery print blouse and fuschia cotton slacks. And again she was barefoot.

"Are you sure you're a naval officer?" he teased as she smiled at him in greeting. It was the first real smile Callie had given him, and he felt the warmth of it flow through him like sunlight across a frozen expanse.

Callie was like the spring sun, slowly dissolving many of the old wounds he'd garnered over the years of his marriage.

Flushing, Callie gestured for him to come in. "Sure. Why?" How handsome he looked in his uniform, she thought. There was a stalwartness to him that she had never noticed in any other man. Perhaps it was the way he squared his shoulders and carried himself so proudly. Or was it the dancing light in his eyes—or the heat that promptly embraced her as he smiled down at her?

"I can't get over the fact that you're a barefoot kind of woman. I'd never have thought it. You really belong in nature, not the navy," he said, smiling back at her as he headed for the kitchen.

Callie shut the door and followed Ty down the hall. Unaccountably, her spirits lifted in his presence. His smile was very male, yet there was a gentleness to it, too. It was a rakish smile, but one that told her that he was genuinely happy to be sharing time with her.

Ty set his garrison cap aside and opened the briefcase. As Callie entered the kitchen, he glanced at her. Her cheeks were flaming red, and he was touched by the knowledge that she wore her feelings so close to the surface. Then, switching to the thought of what Remington had done to her, he truly began to grasp the emotional trauma it had caused Callie. That discovery only made him more angry toward the pilot, but he clamped down on the feeling.

"How is the investigation going?" Callie asked as she poured two glasses of iced tea and set them on the table.

"Interesting," Ty said. He put the briefcase aside and waited for her to sit down.

Once seated, Callie squeezed a fresh slice of lemon into her tea. "Oh? In what way?"

"You remember Lieutenant Clark? The officer who was sitting two tables away from you?"

"Yes?" Callie added several spoonfuls of sugar to her tea and stirred it.

Running his fingers through his hair, Ty muttered, "I talked to him late this morning."

Her hopes rose. "And?"

"He stonewalled me."

"What?" Her heart plummeted. She saw the anger in Ty's eyes and in the grim set of his mouth.

"It was just as you said—ring-knockers stick together."

Laying the spoon on the mat beside her tea, Callie nodded and felt a sadness replace her hope. "I knew it."

"Well, I didn't."

She heard the frustration in Ty's voice and looked over at him. "Now you're getting just a little taste of what will happen. They won't break ranks against the brotherhood, Ty. Not for me. I'm a woman, remember?"

"You're an Annapolis graduate just like them. What about the stuff they pound into us about truth, integrity and honesty—never lying or cheating?"

"Remember? Men have one set of laws, women are treated under a different set?"

Shuffling a bunch of papers together, his eyebrows dipping into a scowl, Ty growled, "I saw it today. Firsthand. I guess I never realized it before. Clark knows a lot, but he's not talking. I went to the O Club and sat at the table where you had your meal that night. I put a tape recorder on Clark's table. Then I talked in a low voice, a medium voice and a loud voice. When I played the tape back, it recorded very clearly at all three tonal levels, so I know Clark not only saw Remington harass you, he heard everything, too."

Admiration for Ty's cleverness made her smile a little. "Maybe you missed your calling."

"How's that?"

"You're a legal eagle at heart."

"I'm good at investigating," he said bluntly, "but I don't think I'd make a very good attorney."

"Why?"

"Because I get too emotionally involved. I *know* you're innocent. You're the victim. I'm angry because we have a witness who could help us, and he's not going to squeal against one of his brothers—even if his brothers are wrong. Frustration is something I'm living with right now, and I'm not a happy camper about how this case is developing."

Callie felt his disgust. "Now you know what we women live with every day of our lives."

"If I were a woman, I'd be changing things in a hurry. I wouldn't take this. Not for a moment."

"If you had been beaten down by a culture that devalues its women the way this one does, you might not have much fight left in you," Callie said softly. She saw Ty give her a confused look. "From the time a woman is born, she's told both verbally and nonverbally that she's not worthy of the same attention, the same importance, the same schooling that a man can get in this country. There are all kinds of studies to prove what I'm saying, Ty. Further, women are taught never to get angry, never to stand up for their rights, and that the only ones who really have rights are men. That's been proven again and again in the courts.

Mothers can't get money from divorced husbands to feed their children—that's just one of many examples."

"I can't say you're wrong about that," he admitted heavily. "But you come out of a family that prided itself on your individuality. Look at Maggie—she's making the military sit up and realize women are capable combat pilots. And I've heard her say that your other two sisters are doing similar things." He gave her a searching look. "Except you. What happened, Callie?"

Uneasily, Callie sipped the tea. "I used to be more like Maggie," she agreed quietly. "But things changed. I changed."

Ty heard the underlying tenor of pain in her voice again. As much as he wanted to dig into that with Callie, he saw the warning in her eyes. Respecting the nonverbal request, he shrugged. "I was planning to call Maggie in before the board on your behalf, and I found out just before I left the office, that they're cutting TAD orders for her to spend the next two weeks doing night landings on a carrier off San Diego."

"What?"

"Yeah, that's what I said."

Callie sat back, feeling utterly defeated. "Someone is pulling strings, Ty. They don't want me to have any witnesses."

"It's beginning to look that way," he said with disgust. He glanced over at the phone. "Any more calls of support today?"

She smiled a little. "Yes, I'm up to twenty-five calls."

With a shake of his head, he muttered, "I never realized how pervasive sexual harassment has become."

"The navy's zero-tolerance policy is a sham," Callie said quietly. "They feed that concept to the public, to the government, but sexual harassment is alive and well in our ranks."

"Well, there won't be a change unless our navy flag officers start giving zero tolerance some teeth. This case could do that."

"Good luck," she murmured.

"Have you gotten any calls from newspapers or television stations?"

"Several, but I've declined all interviews."

"Good. We don't need half truths or portions of our defense broadcast right now."

Rubbing her arms, she said, "I worry a reporter will misquote me—the way they did when Maggie and I did that article for the San Diego newspaper. Look what kind of stink that caused. No, don't worry, I'm not talking to anyone. Except you."

Ty's mouth lifted in a brief smile. "Do you feel a little better about me representing you?"

Callie wanted to tell Ty that he was much more important to her than just that trickle of trust that ebbed and flowed between them. Despite the bad news he'd brought, she still felt safe and protected in his presence. "I do...."

He looked around her kitchen. "This is strictly off the record. We've got a lot of work to do and it will probably take three or four hours to plow through it all." Glancing at his watch, he said, "It's almost dinnertime. How about I take you out to eat? That way, you don't have to hobble around here fixing food for yourself."

Callie suddenly found herself hungry in another way: she wanted the opportunity to get to know Ty Ballard on a personal level. "Do you think if the board gets a hold of the fact that we went to dinner together, it could work against me?"

He shrugged. "Good question. I don't know, Callie. We can always say it was business, not pleasure. Besides, the place I have in mind, a small seaside restaurant down in La Jolla, is off the beaten path of most of these guys."

Her smile broadened. "How did you know I love seafood?"

Ty glanced down at her feet beneath the table. "Any woman who likes to be barefoot has to like sandy beaches."

"You've got a lot more insight than I gave you credit for, Commander Ballard."

"I'll take that as a compliment, Lieutenant Donovan. Well? May I take you to dinner? Afterward, we'll come back to your place and work on the hearing." Never had Ty so much wanted a woman to say yes to his invitation. He saw the joy in Callie's blue eyes and heard the joy in her voice. But he also saw wariness, and some worry. If only he could find out who had made her react this way. If only. . .

"Frankly, I'd like the chance to get out of the house for a while. I'm going a little stir-crazy right now."

"A change of scene is what you need," Ty agreed. *With me.* He hoped his elation hadn't transferred to his face, being all too aware that Callie was particularly sensitive to body language.

"This restaurant, is it a fancy one?"

"No. All you need to do is put on a pair of sandals or shoes and you'll be allowed in the door," he teased.

Her smile was heart-stopping, and Ty gratefully absorbed her momentary happiness. As Callie got to her feet and hobbled out of the kitchen on her crutches, Ty felt life moving through him so strongly that he closed his eyes and savored the intense sensation.

A year of hell had numbed his senses and pulverized his emotions into a nonfeeling state. But whatever it was about Callie, regardless of the pressures on her right now, she affected him deeply. Forever. His unraveling feelings felt like a dam had burst within him, allowing joy to flow through him. Ty took a long, ragged breath. He hadn't believed that Callie would go out with him on a personal invitation. A major miracle had to be at work, he realized, for such a thing to happen.

"What a hell of a bind this is," he muttered as he got to his feet and retrieved his garrison cap. If the situation involving Remington hadn't happened, Ty would never have met Callie. And now he had to defend her at the board hearing. If they lost, it might destroy the relationship he had in mind for them. Callie could, at any point, again perceive him as part of the problem because he was a naval flight officer. That could kill any hope of a relationship, too.

With a shake of his head, he settled the cap on his head and moved to the foyer to wait for Callie. Each moment spent with her had to count. And like a man without water, he found himself thirsting for Callie. More than anything, Ty wanted the dinner to be a positive experience for Callie—and for them.

"I feel like that stuffed lobster I just ate," Callie groaned, patting her stomach. Ty sat across from her in the oak booth appointed with red leather. The restaurant, a laid-back place that was spare and simple, served gourmet-quality food. To be truthful with herself, Callie had to admit that although the food was excellent, Ty's company was the real dessert for her. She'd watched his naval and military image fade to the background during dinner, and the man emerge.

Ty gave her a good-natured look and handed the two large, oval plates to the waitress, who took them away. He wiped his hands on his napkin. "Stuffed is a mild word to describe how much I ate."

"Piggy?"

He chuckled indulgently. "Possibly."

"I ate like one."

Ty held her smiling gaze. "You probably haven't eaten much since all this happened, so you were catching up tonight."

Again, his insight was startling. Since the harassment, Callie had, in fact, eaten very little. She'd had no appetite at all.

The waitress cleared the rest of the table, then brought them each a piece of cheesecake topped with strawberries and a cup of fragrant Colombian coffee.

"When I was a kid growing up in Phoenix, Arizona, I lived out near Luke Air Force Base," Ty told her. "I used to stand next to those huge cyclone fences, hands gripping the wire, watching those birds take off and land. I couldn't get enough of it. All I dreamed of was flying someday."

"Sounds like you started early," Callie commented between bites.

"I guess I did. How about you? Did you dream of a military career?"

With a laugh, Callie said, "Not hardly."

"What did you dream of?"

"Being an artist. Painting." She shrugged. "In a way, I do that now."

"Oh?" Ty was thrilled that she would share some personal information with him.

With a shy smile, Callie said, "On my days off, I take my camera and equipment and go to the seashore to photograph things. I also teach a class on photography at the local college."

"What kind of things?" Ty held his breath, wanting so much for Callie to continue to reveal her real self.

"Oh, you know, tidal pools, pretty clouds that make interesting shapes in the sky, sunsets, the iceplant flowers you find along the cliffs."

"Black-and-white or color photographs?"

"Both." She smiled softly. "I've always dreamed of someday selling a book to a publisher just on seashore topics."

"Why not?"

"Ansel Adams I'm not," she parried wryly, warming beneath his intense interest.

"You could become Callie Donovan, photographer."

"There's not a lot of money to be made in an artistic kind of career."

"Maybe that's true," he hedged, "but you could apply yourself, hang in there and eventually create an opening for your work."

"It's not really that good...."

"Do you have some of your work at home?"

Startled, Callie looked across the table at him. The shadows of the restaurant accented his rugged features, but all she saw in his gray eyes was genuine sincerity and a smoldering warmth that made her feel a little breathless. "Well . . . sure."

Ty glanced at his watch. "It's time we got back, anyway. I'd like to stay here another couple of hours, but that isn't to be. Ready?"

Callie placed a large photo album before Ty. He was sitting at the kitchen table and had refused to start working until she showed him her photos. Nervously, she stood at his shoulder as he opened the album.

"I don't show these to anyone," she murmured, clasping her hands in front of her. "To me, photos are very personal. They tell a great deal about a person, their feelings. . . ."

Ty absorbed the first photo—a color print of a golden sunset with silver lining the puffy cumulus clouds that rose like small turrets above a glassy ocean. The sun's rays shot through the towers of clouds like magical, translucent spokes on a wheel. The effect of the photo was profound and moving. Ty took a deep breath, then glanced up at her.

"This is an outstanding photo. Why should you be nervous about showing this kind of work? It's pretty awesome, if you ask me."

With a slight laugh, Callie shrugged, relieved that at least he didn't think it was awful. "You know how artist types are—they think everything they do is gorgeous. I try to keep a discerning eye on my work. I might take thirty or forty photos, and maybe only one will be worth keeping or working with.''

Ty nodded and turned the page. The next photo was of a little girl, perhaps four years old, in bright red coveralls and a tiny white T-shirt. The child's hair, thin and blond, glinted with sunlight, creating a halolike effect around her head. She was crouched over a tidal pool, a small brown-and-white shell in her hand. Callie had captured the awe in the child's face to perfection. The pool itself was clear, so that a bright red starfish and a purple sea anemone could be seen, like undersea flowers.

"This is incredible," he breathed. "That kid's expression is priceless." Twisting to look up at Callie, he murmured, "You must have spent a long time waiting for just the right moment to snap that."

"Actually, I shot two rolls of film to catch it," she admitted.

"Yes, but you had the patience to wait and watch."

"That's the story of a photographer's life—catching the right moment," she said with a laugh. Thrilled that Ty appreciated her work, Callie began to relax. She pulled a chair up beside him. The next photo was of a woman riding a horse bareback through the ocean surf. "Wow," Ty said, "will you look at this...." He grew quiet, absorbing the photo. The young woman was in her late teens, her hair black as a raven's wing, tinted with bluish highlights as it streamed across her shoulders. The horse she rode at a gallop was also black. The rider wore a green blouse and faded blue Levi's, her feet bare. A look of sheer joy radiated from the woman's face as she leaned forward, the horse's long black mane flowing around her arms and hands. The horse looked equally joyful, with thin, transparent veils of water on either side of him rising in sheets as he galloped full-speed through the shallow ocean surf.

So much in the photo spoke to Ty about Callie. The blue and green of the woman's clothing combined the colors of sky and ocean, making horse and rider a part of the landscape and vice versa. The utter freedom, the abandonment of the moment came across vividly in the photo. He lay his hand across the plastic protecting the print.

"Have you ever ridden a horse?"

"No. I'd like to, but they're pretty big and I'm pretty small. I'm intimidated by size," she murmured, seeing the admiration in Ty's face.

He nodded. Every photo, twelve in all, had a reoccurring theme: freedom and a wild, joyful intensity that affected him deeply. Some were of flowers, others, the ever-changing sky, and others still of women or children. Wanting to see more, he begged Callie to show him the photos she didn't really think were as good.

For the next hour, Ty poured over the huge box of neatly dated and captioned photos. Callie's talent was overwhelming. The obvious sensitivity and care that she put into each shot amazed him. Finally, he set the box aside and just shook his head.

"You're wasting your talent as an Intelligence officer," he muttered. "Those photos are incredible."

She smiled softly. "What did they do for you, Ty?"

"They made me feel. They made me remember back to when I was a kid, or a time when I felt like that woman on the horse—that sense of absolute freedom. You're really something, lady, and I mean that sincerely. I think you ought to send your stuff to magazines, to book publishers. You've got the background—nine years in the navy developing and poring over photos. I mean, what more could a publisher ask?"

His enthusiasm made Callie feel drunk with unexpected happiness. The burning light in his gaze drew her, and she wondered blankly what it would be like to kiss that strong, smiling mouth, to be enveloped in his intensity, the passion he so obviously felt for life.

Her mouth suddenly dry, she got to her feet and nervously took the box and set it on the counter. "Maybe someday I'll do those things," she said. "I just don't feel I'm good enough yet. I see the flaws in my photos."

Frowning, Ty watched her come back to the table and sit down. The real Callie Donovan was an earthy, breathtaking creature with a sense of whimsy—and a shyness he couldn't understand. Forcing himself back to the business at hand, he growled, "For my money, you're already a professional photographer. All you lack is enough belief in yourself to do it."

"That's the confident jet jock talking," Callie retorted with a laugh. "But thanks for looking at them. It's nice to be appreciated for something other than being able to look at microscopic details on a satellite photo."

Ty wanted to appreciate Callie in a lot of ways. Without thinking, he reached across the table and captured her tightly clasped hands. "You remind me of a butterfly that's trapped in a chrysalis, Callie. I see the freedom in your photos. And I wonder how much freedom has been taken away from you."

Shaken, Callie looked down at the table, feeling the heat from Ty's hand enveloping her own cool ones. "My freedom was taken away from me a long time ago," she choked out.

Chapter Eight

Ty slowly removed his hand from Callie's, all the while holding her unsteady gaze. She was nervous. Terribly nervous. And the pain in her tone made him wince inwardly. Taking a breath, he decided to broach the topic. Callie trusted him, he hoped, enough to level with him. The fact that she'd entrusted her beautiful photos, expressions of her most intimate self with him was the sign he'd needed.

"Look," he began heavily, "I get the feeling there's something tragic in your background, Callie." He pointed to the reports. "If it has any bearing on this hearing, we need to discuss it."

Callie sat very still, her heart plummeting with fear—and shame. Under no circumstances could Ty learn of the humiliation that had been done to her at Annapolis. "No," she whispered, "I don't want to talk about it."

Remaining very calm and trying not to overreact to her decision, he said, "If it has anything to do with what's happened, Callie, I should know about it. Don't you think?"

The pain tearing through Callie's gut almost made her bend over. She wrapped her arms protectively around her stomach and refused to look at Ty. The tenor of his voice was kind and searching, and she knew that he was trying to be sensitive to her needs.

"I...no, I just can't, Ty. Please, don't press this issue." She glanced apprehensively up at him, to see his face set and grim. "Let's just stick to this incident. It's enough." Her voice cracked with sudden emotion. "It's more than enough for me to handle."

Searching her shadowed blue eyes, Ty sensed her pain as if it were tangible. Mentally, he went back to Callie's precious photos, the statement of her as a human being, and as a woman. The photos were about nature, about children and mothers. He hadn't seen a photo of a male, adult or child. Looking deeply into her eyes, he tried to ferret out why. There was such fear in her face that he didn't know what to do or say.

Rubbing his jaw, rough with beard this late in the evening, he muttered, "You know that the defense will bring up your Annapolis record. Nothing is sacred in this hearing, Callie. If there's anything in your background that they can use against you, they'll do it."

"I have no doubt," she retorted, obviously rattled. "But you see, my record is spotless. I was a 4.0 for four years. I graduated fourth out of my entire class. They won't find anything to hang me with if that's what you're worried about."

Ty cocked his head, hearing the tightly held anger laced with a brittleness that made him sense she was very close to breaking into tears. "Okay," he whispered and held up his hand in a sign of peace. "I'll back off." *For now.*

Relief, sharp and dizzying, cut through Callie. Rubbing her brow, she forced back the tears that clogged her throat. Shame moved through her, and she found herself trapped in the past. The photos had stirred memories, too. Hard as she tried, she couldn't stop the tears from forming behind her closed lids.

"Excuse me," she said abruptly, getting up and leaving the kitchen as quickly as possible. Reaching the refuge of her bedroom, Callie shut the door. Hating the crutches, she threw them on the carpeted floor and hobbled under her own power to her bed. There she sat down and grabbed a tissue from the box on the bedstand. Tears began leaking, unchecked, from her tightly shut eyes.

As much as Callie wanted Ty to be holding her, she couldn't ask that of him. Although he was slowly mending her trust, in a larger perspective he still represented what had happened, and she couldn't shake that knowledge—at least, not yet. Sitting on the bed, quietly sobbing, Callie realized just how lonely she really was. Ty provided such a powerful sense of intimacy and nurturance for her starved, beaten emotions.

Callie sat for a good half hour after crying, thinking long and hard about Ty Ballard. He had a past, too, she realized. In fact, his reputation preceded him, and she'd nearly damned him for that. But despite his less-than-glorious reputation, he'd turned out to be a decent human being. Confused, Callie shook her head. Her whole life seemed to be changing with such frightening speed that she didn't know how to act or respond.

When she finally returned to the kitchen—without her crutches, because she refused to continue to feel so crippled—Ty had made coffee, poured himself a cup, and was at work. At first, immersed in the report, he didn't notice her, and Callie had a rare precious moment to observe him, to appreciate him and his efforts. Then, although she'd made no sound or movement, it was as if he suddenly, on some subconscious level, sensed her presence.

Ty jerked his head up and his eyes widened at the sight of Callie standing brokenly before him. Her shoulders were slumped, her hands hung at her sides and her eyes were rimmed in red. Putting his pencil aside, he scraped back his chair and rose. He wasn't thinking, only feeling, as he rounded the table and headed for her. Her grief-filled eyes beckoned him, and throwing caution aside, he reached out as he approached Callie.

Taking her hands in his, he halted inches from where she stood with such uncertainty. She took in a ragged gasp of air at his touch, but she didn't jump away from him. In fact, she didn't try to pull out of his grip at all. She tried to smile but failed terribly, her mouth pursed, still holding back some unknown anguish.

"I'm sorry," he rasped thickly. "I didn't know you were crying or I'd—" He halted. He'd have done what? Gone to her? Held her? Ty swallowed hard and shrugged. The very fact that Callie had run from him, not asking for his help, told him the bitter truth: she still didn't trust him when the cards were on the table.

But somehow the rejection didn't matter, and Ty followed his instincts.

Leaning down, he cupped her face in his hands and drowned in her luminous eyes, which were shadowed with sorrow. Breathing out her name, feeling as if he was taking a risk bigger than any navy dog fight, Ty moved still closer and gently touched his lips to hers. She tasted salty, he thought abstractly, and he realized, in some far compartment of his mind that was rapidly spinning out of control, that he was tasting the salt of her spent tears.

Nothing could have made him more tender than that discovery as he moved his mouth coaxingly across hers, silently asking her to return his searching kiss. He felt Callie breathe in raggedly, her hands moving against his chest, and then her mouth responded. There was such exquisite beauty as her lips molded more surely to his own, and joy—white-hot and blinding—seared through him. Her mouth was soft and firm, giving and taking, against his own. The sweet taste of her as a woman filled him, and Ty groaned, the sound reverberating throughout his tense body.

The raggedness of Callie's breathing, moist and featherlike across his cheek, told him that she was equally stunned by the intensity of the kiss. Fighting a desire to become more aggressive, to take and drink more deeply from her, Ty honored his sense of how fragile their kiss was—and what it could mean to their future. And how he wanted a future with Callie, he admitted suddenly as he eased his mouth from hers. Watching her thick lashes slowly open, discovering the hazy blueness of her eyes touched with gold, he smiled tenderly.

The moment was like a breathtaking rainbow for Ty as he held her warm gaze banked with desire, more than aware of the tremulous smile that touched the corners of her mouth. Taking a deep breath, he moved his hands gently from her face.

"I didn't know what else to do," he said thickly, his hands coming to rest on her shoulders. "You were hurting."

The sound of his voice, deep and ragged, moved over Callie like a lover's hands. At a loss for words, she understood why Ty had kissed her. She had kissed him back, no less in need than he. Heat ebbed and flowed through her, and all she could do was stand and feel his masculine power, feel the steadying touch of his grip on her shoulders. The kiss Ty had given her was intended to heal her—not to take from her, as so many others had been.

Closing her eyes, she moved her hand tentatively across his chest, feeling his muscles tighten beneath her flowing touch. "I..." She gulped, a flood of need shearing through her. Stunned by her hunger for Ty, Callie lifted her head and met his blazing eyes, which burned with a hunger to match her own. "I never expected it...."

With a one-cornered smile, Ty said, "I didn't, either." Each strand of her black hair was thick and silky beneath his continued caresses. "I'm sorry I made you cry. I feel really bad. I shouldn't have pushed you the way I did."

With a shake of her head, Callie knew she had to move away from Ty or kiss him again. His sheer maleness was overwhelming her spinning senses, and she didn't dare capitulate, even though she wanted to. "It's all right," she rasped, and disengaged herself from his embrace. "It happened a long time ago. I just want to forget it, that's all."

Ty tried to swallow his disappointment as Callie stepped away from him. Her cheeks had flushed bright red, and he knew that what they'd just shared had been utterly spontaneous on both their parts. Still, his spirit soared with the revelation that Callie had kissed him back—so there was hope. He moved farther away to give her the space to feel safe again. "Well, I'm here if you ever need a friend's shoulder to cry on. Okay?"

"Okay...." Callie moved around Ty, because if she didn't, she was going to step forward and throw her arms around his strong neck and broad, capable shoulders. The stormy craving in his gray eyes, touched her as little else could. She felt his longing for her, and it was a wonderful sensation, despite the underlying fear it aroused. Puttering at the counter, trying to control the nervousness she felt, Callie poured herself a cup of coffee. She heard Ty move back to the table and sit down.

Once, as she rinsed some dishes and loaded them into the dishwasher, she stole a quick glance in his direction. His generous mouth was set, like a dam withholding unspoken feelings. His dark eyebrows were gathered like thunderclouds as he worked doggedly in the silence. Feeling shaky, Callie returned to her kitchen work, relieved that Ty wasn't going to press the issue of their unexpected kiss.

Finally, half an hour later, Ty called her over to the table. He showed her the outline of his presentation to the board and asked for her input. Although she was trying to concentrate, Callie found it nearly impossible. The chaos of her emotions combined with Ty's quiet strength and stability to conspire against her. She sat down, pressing her hands to her brow as she read his neatly printed outline.

"A psychiatrist?" she murmured in surprise, and looked up at him.

He smiled a little. "Yes. I called up the San Diego psychiatric association and asked if there was anyone who was an expert on sexual harassment in their ranks." Pleased with himself, he jabbed a finger at the name. "Dr. Marlene Johnson is a nationally recognized expert on the topic. She's frequently called in as an expert witness in cases involving sexual harassment."

"How do we pay her?"

"We don't. I told her what was going down, and she volunteered her services and time on your behalf. I explained that under the rules of the UCMJ, we couldn't pay her anything, and I think she recognizes that the problems in the military are pretty overwhelming."

"So she'll get cross-examined, too."

Ty grinned a bit more widely. "Yes. This lady is sharp. She's cool under fire and knows her subject, so I feel that no matter what the other counsels do, they won't shake her in the least."

"Unlike me," Callie said. "I'm not so sure I can be calm and cool when I get grilled by those counsels. I'm angry, and when I get like that, I physically start to shake. My voice trembles, and I unravel."

"Don't worry about it," Ty said in a reassuring voice, although he was worried about that very thing. If Callie behaved like a stereotypical "hysterical woman," it would count against her with the board. Tears and high emotions were foreign to the navy. He patted her hand. "I'm going to set up an appointment for both of us to talk with her tomorrow, if that's okay with you."

Callie nodded. "Sure, it's fine. Frankly, I can use all the support I can get. Now that Lieutenant Clark has refused to help me, my case doesn't have a leg to stand on. It's three witnesses against my word. And I know Remington and those other two pilots are meeting together daily to get their story straight, so you can't poke holes in it and expose them."

"That's why I searched out an expert," Ty said reassuringly. "Dr. Johnson will give us back what we lost in Clark."

Callie gave him a warm look filled with undeniable pride. "You continually surprise me. You just aren't anything like I thought you'd be."

"Can't judge a book by the cover, can you?" Ty teased lightly. How badly he wanted to kiss Callie again—only this time, a long, deep, slow kiss that would melt them into a burning fire of oneness. Reluctantly, he forced himself back to the issues at hand. "Or maybe I should say, you can judge a photo by its cover?"

Laughing a little, feeling a bit of relief, Callie agreed, "I didn't know you would get so much out of my photos."

"I got a lot," Ty assured her huskily. "More than you'll ever realize."

She sat back and tried to relax. "What did you find out?"

He smiled and set the pencil aside. "That you really are a nature lover. You're happiest around the ocean, because it gives you that sense of freedom you don't feel otherwise, for some unknown reason." He saw her face quickly close up, and went on in a light tone, hoping to draw her back out. "It's obvious you love children—about half the photos are of them. And I think you like to play like a child, even if you don't get a chance to exercise that side of yourself very often. Everything in your photos speaks of peace, not harm or violence."

Alarmed, Callie began to realize just how much Ty had seen of her through the photos. His gaze now was dark and intense—one that made her wildly aware of herself as a woman. Somehow, he'd discovered the essence of her—the fact that despite the tragedy that dogged her heels, she received a quiet strength and renewal through Mother Earth and nature.

His look seemed as palpable as a lover's touch, and the sensation was electric, moving through her like ribbons wafting on the wind. Desire, like a storm suddenly moving inland off the ocean, shot through Callie. She was caught by the smoldering gray of his eyes, nakedly proclaiming his hunger for her. More surprisingly, she felt a hunger within her to equal his. The realization shocked her, and she quickly dropped her gaze, her heart pounding madly in her breast.

Shaken by the discovery, by the real and sizzling needs boiling through her blood, Callie couldn't speak. She could only feel—deeply, vibrantly. Ty hadn't touched her, yet her entire body and heart had responded to that one very male look he'd shared with her. Could one kiss have so unhinged her. Made her feel primal? Confused, Callie found her voice.

"I—I'm really tired. Can we call it a night?"

"Sure." Unwillingly Ty gathered up all the papers, feeling the tightness of his need for her. Callie was like a siren—a mermaid come to land in a woman's body. There was such an ethereal, haunting quality to her.

His hands trembling slightly as he repacked the information in his briefcase, Ty felt the delicious throbbing tension in the kitchen. That one wide-eyed look of hers, her beautiful turquoise eyes meeting and holding his gaze, had triggered an incredible amount of longing within him.

He wanted Callie—in every way. Yes, he wanted to feel her against him, he wanted to explore her wildly with kisses and revel in her response. There was no denying he wanted to find her in his arms, in his bed, at his side. But there was so much more, Ty admitted. How he longed to walk hand in hand with her along a sandy beach and simply watch her blossom beneath less-harsh, less-militaristic conditions.

As he rose, he wondered exactly what price Callie had paid to remain in the navy. A heavy one, he acknowledged. She belonged barefoot, her camera in hand, in the wilds of the world—not in some darkened room for twelve-hour shifts looking at tiny, microscopic objects to identify as military targets. What a waste, he thought, as he eased around the table. It was as if navy life had sucked the lifeblood out of her, and the only way she could recapture even part of it was in her stunning photos.

"I'll call you tomorrow around 0800 and let you know when I'll pick you up to meet with Dr. Johnson."

Callie gazed up at Ty. He was so near that she could feel that incredible aura of confidence and strength that always surrounded him. "Yes." She reached out and briefly touched his forearm. "Thanks—for everything, Ty. Good night...."

It took every shred of Ty's discipline and good sense to leave. Callie was worn down by tonight's interaction with him. Her skin looked almost translucent, stretched tautly over her cheekbones—evidence of the emotional price she'd paid to reach out and trust him.

"Good night," he rasped. Turning abruptly, he left, before he stayed and made the worst mistake of his life.

Marriage to Jackie had taught him a great many things—among them, that a woman craved a natural intimacy with her man. As Ty shut the car door and strapped on the seat belt, he was deep in thought. Jackie had taught him that a woman liked to talk with her man—on an intimate level, not just about what had happened during the day at work. He'd come to appreciate that in his ex-wife, and he knew without a doubt that Callie would benefit from it, too—as would he.

But Callie was fragile in a way Jackie never had been. And Ty was at a loss about how to handle it—or what to do without blowing the trust he'd managed to build between them.

Grousing to himself, Ty drove away from the apartment complex, very unhappy and yet in another way euphoric. That one galvanizing look had held so much heat and promise, riveting both of them into a mute stare. Sweet God, but he'd savored that moment like a man with a raging thirst finally being fed drops of life-giving water. And now he knew that Callie was also drawn to him. He'd seen the expression in her face, the beauty in her eyes. And their kiss. He groaned loudly. Yes, there was something there to build upon.

Whistling softly, Ty paid only cursory attention to the late-evening traffic around him. Nor did he pay any mind to the avenues of palms or the pale lavender tint to the sky just before the cloak of darkness unfolded across the land. On every level his awareness was focused on his emotions toward Callie. There was such richness to her that he felt like a gold miner who'd just discovered a tunnel bearing the valuable mineral. Only Callie wasn't to be mined in some greedy, selfish way.

Ty saw himself being able to appreciate her in ways he'd never been able to appreciate another woman— not even his ex-wife. Callie had many layers—surprising layers that she slowly, with coaxing, was revealing to him. And this was just the beginning, he realized with pleasure. If only this hearing wasn't hanging over her—and him—and the relationship he was cultivating despite the threat of it.

Some of his happiness eroded as he considered the secret that Callie carried deep within her heart and soul. Something had happened back at Annapolis. Something tragic. Something she insisted wasn't in her personnel record. What could it be? Had she fallen in love with a young man who'd died? Or dumped her? Or had she had a series of men who'd never appreciated her, ending up scorned and mortally wounded by the combined experiences?

Ty knew how rough the navy was on men, and he was beginning to get an inkling of how much rougher it could be on women. He sensed that Maggie, Callie's sister, thrived on the challenge that the navy threw like a gauntlet in her face. But Callie wasn't of the same temperament. Maggie was decidedly an extrovert and assertive—a natural leader. Callie was an introvert, a follower—and an artist at heart. The navy would never appreciate what Callie brought to the service.

The next few days leading up to the board hearing were going to be nerve-racking for Callie. Ty wished he could protect her, but it was impossible. Callie's armor, that tough side he was sure had been born in the heat of whatever battles she'd endured at Annapolis, would have to be erected to help her remain steady and cool. Ty had seen that side of her briefly when she'd challenged him. She would have to find that same scrappy defiance and anger, and fuse it into an impenetrable shield to protect her from the attacks to come.

"Dammit," he whispered as he turned onto the street leading to his home. Without a doubt, he knew that the three counsels would do their level best not only to gut Callie in front of the board, but to wound her mortally, if possible. They'd do it to teach not only her a lesson, but every other woman who had even a second thought about bringing an officer under scrutiny for sexual harassment. No, they were going to make Callie a scapegoat, and Ty felt an inner rage— and an inner need to protect her at all costs from such an attack.

His hands tightening on the steering wheel, Ty braked the car and turned into the driveway of his ranch-style home, placed elbow-to-elbow in a row of similar houses. Turning off the ignition, he unlatched his seat belt and opened the door.

Getting out of the sports car, Ty walked slowly toward the entrance, fishing in his pocket for his house-keys, deep in thought. That retired navy captain-turned-attorney would make mincemeat out of his toddling attempts to protect Callie. He wondered if the board would allow the pack of opposing counsels to viciously and continuously assail Callie. Opening the door to his house, Ty flipped on the living room light. Dropping his briefcase on the bamboo-style couch, he wandered into the small but neat kitchen.

Going to the refrigerator, he pulled out a cold beer and opened it. Unlocking the rear door, Ty moseyed out to the patio and sat down on the lounger. Taking a long sip of beer, he looked up at the sky. Thin gray clouds were quickly covering what few stars were visible in the sky filled with San Diego's reflected light. Was it symbolic? he wondered. The stratus moved like dark, silent fingers across the sky, gobbling up everything in their path.

Worried, his heart and mind settled back on Callie and her plight. He wanted to protect her not because he didn't think she was capable of protecting herself, but because he liked her and wanted to keep her safe. He smiled a little to himself.

"You've got it bad, Ballard. If anyone knew The Predator had just tripped head over heels for a woman, they'd laugh themselves to death over it," he muttered aloud to the darkening night sky. Ty had known Jackie for two years before he'd married her— wanting to make sure she was the right woman for him. Well, time hadn't been much of a guarantee, he thought, smiling derisively. Stunned by how much Callie now lived and breathed through each pore of him, Ty shook his head in wonderment. She was such a petite little thing—but he'd seen that Donovan backbone of steel once or twice, too.

Maybe they did have a chance at the board—albeit a slim one. So much hinged on how Callie held herself together under fire. If she could come across as tough, resilient and relentless, then the men on the board might respect her—and believe her over the three pilots whom Ty knew would lie to save their careers at her expense.

Gripping the cool, moisture-beaded bottle of beer, Ty leaned back, suddenly exhausted. He felt as if lightning had nailed him tonight after that kiss with Callie. His emotions were reeling, but he had to scramble to remain coherent, focused and intense for Callie's sake. Releasing a breath, Ty wished the day for the hearing would hurry up and come. Callie was suffering badly, the torture of waiting taking a toll on her—as it was on him, too. No, next Monday couldn't come soon enough.

Chapter Nine

Callie took one last look in the mirror of the women's lavatory located in the Operations building at Miramar. Her hands were damp and sweaty, and her heart wouldn't settle down. It was Monday morning, and in five minutes the board would be convened in a room adjacent to the teaching facility.

She stared at herself critically. Her hair, washed last night, fell neatly, straight and thick. The white blouse and skirt were starched and pressed to perfection. The black boards with two gold stripes sat on each of her small shoulders, making them appear even more thrown back than usual. Normally, she wore black heels with the uniform, but because of her healing ankle, the only thing she could possibly wear were her black "boondockers," which looked more like granny shoes, their black patent leather shining like mirrors on her feet.

Callie had resisted Ty's idea of facing the board with her ankle wrapped in the Ace bandage. She might limp, but she wasn't going to look like a cripple. No way. For the thousandth time, she wished Maggie was here, but as Ty had warned, her sister had been sent away on carrier duty, practicing night landings at sea. Right now, she could use some of Maggie's strength and passionate belief about what was right and wrong in the world.

Although she wore no makeup, Callie had put on a bit of perfume as she did every morning. The subtle, spicy fragrance had nearly worn off and she wasn't going to replenish it for this. She avoided looking at the faint darkness beneath her eyes.

She washed her hands in an attempt to get rid of the clammy feeling, then dried them on a paper towel. She knew that she'd meet the perpetrators outside the room and all of them would go in together. Because of the ankle injury, she hadn't had to go back to work last week and face Remington. Just thinking about seeing him again tied her stomach in knots.

The only sliver of hope, of stability, that she had was the thought of Ty Ballard. His enthusiasm, his belief in her and the rightness of her case had held her together. Without him, Callie knew she'd have sunk to a level of cowardice even she would have been ashamed to admit to. Instead, she'd absorbed his quiet but powerful strength and used it as her own. Somehow, she hadn't found the energy or fight to erect her own armor, as Ty referred to it.

Taking a deep, ragged breath, she turned and left the restroom. At 0800, the halls were empty, the Top Gun students already in class, and for that she was grateful. Right now, Callie couldn't stand the leering stares, the accusation in the pilots' eyes. She knew from several other women officers that her name and the charges brought to bear against Remington and the others had been a hot topic of gossip all over the station. Callie was glad she hadn't had to hear it first-hand.

Walking with a slight limp, the pain still very real in her ankle, Callie turned the corner and saw a group of navy officers in summer white uniforms crowded around the door. Her heart hammered fiercely in her chest as they collectively stopped talking and turned to stare at her. Her mouth going dry, Callie reached deep within herself and forced herself to walk with at least some note of confidence despite her limp.

Out of the crowd stepped Ty Ballard. His gray eyes zeroed in on hers, and she felt their instant rapport as he walked toward her. She had driven to the station in her own car and hadn't seen him yet. Today, he wasn't his normal warm, effusive self. Instead, his eyes were dark with an unfamiliar intensity, his mouth grim. This was the warrior side of him, Callie reminded herself as she approached him. She felt the angry stares of the other officers—felt them as surely as if they were invisible barbs being hurled in her direction.

She tried to dismiss the presence of the men who had hurt her, who had deliberately attacked her, but all she felt was rage and a shakiness deep within herself. As Ty slowed to a stop, he reached out, his hand connecting with her elbow briefly as he moved her to one side of the passageway. His touch was soothing. A part of her instantly relaxed, and she halted, her back to the rest of the group.

"Hi," Ty murmured. He forced himself to break contact with Callie. Anything other than unquestionably official behavior between them could be held against her, so he had to stay on top of his instinctive need to protect her.

Callie's mouth quirked. "Hi."

He searched her pale face. "You get any sleep last night?"

"No. Did you?"

"A little," Ty lied. Actually, he'd stayed up almost all night preparing questions for Remington based on the psychiatrist's suggestions. Toward 0400, he'd lain down, caught two hours of sleep, then had got up, showered, shaved and gone over to the station.

Callie desperately wanted to wrap her arms protectively around herself, but to do so would wrinkle her uniform, and she didn't want that. "I'm scared, Ty."

"You're going to be fine. I've got one hell of a defense for you, thanks to Dr. Johnson." He smiled a little, then looked up to study the group. "The three commanders are already in the hearing room. In another minute or so, the shore-patrol guard will open the doors and we can go in."

"Do I have to sit next to them?"

"We'll let them go in first and then we'll follow," Ty murmured. He saw the terror in her eyes, but hopefully no one else would. Callie's nervousness did show up in her darting glances, although she stood very still, as if aware her body language might give her away to the enemy.

She released a long sigh. "Okay, good. I—I just want to get this over with."

"You know it's going to take two or three days, don't you?"

Shutting her eyes momentarily, Callie nodded. "You mentioned that." She opened her eyes and stared up at Ty's composed, rugged features. "Aren't you scared?"

"No."

"You look so calm, cool and collected," she muttered defensively.

"The only time my hands shake is when I'm making a cat take-off or landing on a carrier at night. Then they shake like hell."

Giving him an accusing look, she said, "I might have known your jet-jock arrogance would come out now."

"At least it's on your side," he whispered with a smile. Her lips were soft and inviting, and Ty held himself very tightly in check, longing to kiss her, to reassure her.

Rubbing her arm, Callie nodded. "I feel like I'm going to explode inside. I want to run. I want to hide."

Battling the urge to touch her, to somehow soothe the panic so clearly written in her eyes, Ty said, "We're a team, you and I. This is *our* fight. We'll do what they did in medieval times—put our backs against each other and let the enemy encircle us, swords drawn. That way, we can see them coming no matter which direction they charge from."

Smiling a little at the image, Callie muttered, "You really are a throwback, Ballard. Straight back to the days of King Arthur. All you need is your white horse, and you'd be set."

He grinned and said, "My white horse is an F-14 Tomcat."

"I feel more like I'm Sancho Panza and you're Don Quixote, and we're both tilting at windmills."

At that moment Ty didn't care who was looking, although he kept his gesture discreet and brief. Reaching out, he captured her hand, which was damp and cold, and squeezed it warmly. "You be the pessimist and I'll be the optimist. We'll get through this one minute at a time."

His touch was like a healing balm soothing the ragged terror stabbing at Callie's midsection. Giving Ty a grateful look, she said, "You deserve someone a lot more heroic than me. I'm a coward at heart."

"So was the lion in *The Wizard of Oz* until he was given a heart." Ty held her sad blue eyes, fraught with anxiety. "I'll be your heart if you let me, Callie. I'll fight for you because I believe your story, and I believe in you."

Callie didn't have time to answer, because just then the doors to the hearing room opened. Instantly, she felt Ty's hand on her arm, cautioning her to remain still. Taking those precious seconds, Callie tried to calm herself. She had to pretend to be cool and disconnected emotionally—just as she had back at Annapolis. Somehow, it was tougher this time to force that cauldron of emotions to the place deep inside herself where she'd stored it through her academy days.

Ty's reassuring presence helped her walk, although her knees felt weak. Callie remembered that same feeling after the terrible incident at Annapolis. For nearly six months after the fact she'd felt just this wobbly, and she wasn't surprised the sensation had returned. Wasn't she being attacked again despite all the official trappings?

The three-person board sat at the front of the room on a raised dais of dark, highly polished maple. The commanders looked grim and somber in their summer white uniforms, not allowing an inkling of what they were feeling to show on their faces. The fluorescent lights made the rectangular room appear almost surrealistic to Callie. In the center stood a wooden chair, where the person being questioned would be seated. To the right was a row of chairs, extending from one end of the room to the other. A court stenographer, an enlisted Wave who had a yeoman-first-class rating, sat to the left of the tribunal. The Wave appeared to be in her early thirties and if Callie's eyes didn't deceive her, the blond-haired woman gave her a brief look of camaraderie.

Ty guided Callie to the middle of the room. Remington and his gang had grabbed the chairs closest to the tribunal next to the window. That was fine by him; he wanted the center, where he could see everyone's faces, including those of the board. He was mildly surprised that Remington wasn't in his usual top form, tossing verbal innuendos and giving Callie—or for that matter, the yeoman—leering looks. Obviously his counsel, Jason Lewis, the retired navy attorney, had been teaching him more proper manners in order to win the case. Well, it wasn't going to work if Ty could help it.

As Callie sat down, Ty spotted Dr. Johnson at the door. He straightened and gestured for her to come in. The woman was in her early fifties, with streaks of silver among the dark strands of her short hair. Compared to the spit-and-polish image of everyone else in the room, Dr. Johnson seemed like a colorful, beautiful flower. She wore a ballet-length hot pink cotton skirt and a tasteful Venetian white blouse with a bright yellow blazer over it.

Ty curbed a smile as he saw Remington's eyes nearly pop out of his head at the appearance of the slender, beautiful Dr. Johnson. Remington caught himself only after Lewis jabbed him discreetly in the ribs with his elbow. Instantly the pilot jerked his head around, feigning ignorance of Dr. Johnson's dramatic entrance. As Ty walked over and extended his hand to the psychiatrist, he didn't miss the interest in the faces of the three commanders who composed the tribunal. Everything about Marlene Johnson was movement— from her long, flowing skirt to the drape of her oversize blazer and the colorful scarf that trailed halfway to the floor from around her neck. Tasteful gold earrings and a choker necklace emphasized her dancing, brown eyes as she smiled and gripped Ty's hand.

"Good morning, Commander. I'm a bit late. Traffic."

"You're right on time," he murmured. "Come and sit down next to Lieutenant Donovan."

Dr. Johnson smiled at Callie as she sat down. "You look ready," she told her in a low, confident voice.

Callie felt every set of eyes in the room on them. Whether it was true or not, she didn't dare look up to find out. Instead, she focused on Dr. Johnson's undeniable warmth and upbeat greeting. "I'm glad, because I have to be."

"You'll do fine. Just remember my coaching."

Callie nodded. In the last two days, Dr. Johnson had spent several hours with Callie and Ty, prepping them for responses to the charges that were sure to come, the denials and the accusations from the pilots. As far as Callie was concerned, Dr. Johnson was a role model for all women, with the unmistakable freedom she exuded and the irrepressible vitality in her eyes and voice. Calie felt dead in comparison; she had come close to telling Dr. Johnson about Annapolis, about that other dark period in her life. At the last moment, though, she'd backed out, fearful that she'd be judged harshly.

"Attention!" the guard announced in a loud, rolling voice.

Everyone came to attention except Dr. Johnson.

"At ease," Commander Newton, the head of the tribunal, said. He cracked the gavel once, the sound echoing like a shot through the room. Newton, who had gray hair and caterpillarlike eyebrows, shot a look in Ty's direction.

"Commander Ballard, please present Lieutenant Donovan's case. You may call any witnesses or corroborative testimony that you feel supports her charges of sexual harassment."

Ty rose and moved smoothly to the center of the room, notepad in hand. "Thank you, sir. I'd like to call Dr. Marlene Johnson, psychiatrist, to the stand."

Callie watched Dr. Johnson move as lightly as a feather on the wind. Out of the corner of her eye she could see Remington's face take on that familiar hungry look as the psychiatrist moved to the chair, then repeated the oath to tell the truth that the yeoman read to her. Disgust filled her. As Ty began to ask Dr. Johnson to explain her background as an internationally recognized expert on sexual harassment, Callie divided her attention between Ty and the doctor, and the pilots who sat stoic and emotionless.

"Dr. Johnson, I know that most men will say that sexual harassment is harmless fun," Ty said, glancing over at the wall of pilots. "What is your psychological assessment?"

"First of all," the doctor replied in a low, husky tone, "there are a number of common attitudes expressed by the victimizer. I won't go into those just yet, but I want this board to realize that unwanted sexual attentions hurt the victim. It's not a targetless game that's being played. Harassment can't exist without a target at which it is aimed, and the goal is to inflict attention that isn't wanted by the woman—in this case, Lieutenant Donovan."

"But," Ty said, playing devil's advocate, "I'm sure these officers are going to tell you that it's harmless attention, not meant to hurt anyone."

Marlene Johnson became grim. She aimed her index finger at the pilots. "I'd like to remind everyone in this room that the offender or offenders are not the ones capable of defining who is and is not hurt. Only the victim is."

Smiling inwardly, Ty nodded. Score one for their side. He saw the tribunal react to Johnson's logic. "Be kind enough to outline for all of us, Doctor, the various levels of sexual harassment."

"First," Marlene said briskly, touching her index finger to begin the count, "there is what is known as 'nonaggressive appreciation.' In a layperson's terms, it's called aesthetic appreciation. What this means is that the harasser has a physical or sexual appreciation of the target. He sets himself up to be superior in that he's judging the target's physical attributes. Another course of action he may take is to trivialize the target's professionalism by making comments about the target's physical or sexual attributes. This is often done by the harasser when a lot of men are around, and the target is outnumbered."

"Can you give us an example of this?"

"Sure. If one of these men says, 'Lieutenant Donovan, you look *great* in your uniform,' that's harassment."

"Why?"

"Because no male officer would go up to another male officer and say, 'You look *great* in your uniform.' To do so would be to risk his heterosexual reputation." She smiled a little as the pilots moved uncomfortably. "The key here is that it's harassment if you can't say it to either gender. In other words, you are singling out an individual and being discriminatory, no matter how harmless the compliment may seem to the harasser."

"And the second level?" Ty prompted. He glanced over at Callie, who looked wan and tense.

"It's a more aggressive level of borderline sexual harassment and is termed 'active mental groping.' Things such as continual staring at the target, or at some part of her anatomy, such as her breasts or legs, is an example of this type of harassment in action. Or the harasser may stand over or behind the woman in order to look down the front of her blouse or dress. That's the nonverbal type. The verbal type would say something like, 'What you need is a good lay to straighten you out.'"

Ty saw Remington wince. Good, he thought, again wanting to smile. The bastard should know what he'd been doing for so many years. "And the third level, Dr. Johnson?"

"'Social touching.' Harassment goes from being nonverbal or verbal to actual physical touching of the target. At this level, men deliberately plot to rub up against or come up behind their target. They'll catch her in the elevator and purposely bump into her, but it will look like an accident. Of course, it's not. Another determining aspect of this is how it feels to the target—friendly versus sensual. Of course, the harasser always intends a sensual touch."

"And the fourth level?"

Marlene crossed her legs. "This is the stage where the harasser becomes bolder and moves beyond 'accidental' touching, actively and purposefully going out of his way to make deliberate contact. This man will drape his arm around the woman and then brush his hand along the side of her breast. Or, if his hand is resting on her waist, he'll inch it up toward her breast or down across her buttocks to get a 'feel.' The harasser will deliberately touch her breast without seemingly doing anything improper—again, as if it were accidental."

"There's a great deal of deliberateness about the harasser doing this, isn't there, Doctor?"

"Actually," she responded with a grimace, "I equate a harasser of this variety as a predator knowingly and consciously stalking his intended victim. It's not casual. It's not accidental. It's planned from start to finish."

"And the final level, Doctor. What kind of harasser is he?"

"Actually, there are two types in the last category, Commander. The fifth level is what is considered taboo social behavior, such as grabbing and trying to kiss his target, groping for her breasts and not being deterred no matter what she does to stop him. The physical attention is forced upon the target."

"And the last kind?"

"The worst," Marlene Johnson muttered. "The sixth-level harasser, in effect, tells the target to go to bed with him, or put out in some way, or lose her job. In essence, it is physical and/or psychological rape of the target. She has to give this sick harasser sex and keep quiet about what he's doing to her, or she won't get a raise, a promotion, or even keep her job."

Callie saw the anger on Remington's face. He had more than once suggested she go to bed with him or suffer the consequences. And Marlene Johnson's absolute disgust at this type of man was having quite an effect on the tribunal, judging from the looks on their faces.

Callie's heart picked up a beat, because she knew she would be called next. Ty had figured that her testimony would last until lunchtime. Then there would be a two-hour break and she would face the cross-examination of the three counsels for the rest of the day—and perhaps into tomorrow.

Ty thanked Dr. Johnson and called Callie to the stand. He kept his expression carefully neutral as she limped up to the chair and placed her hand on the Bible carried forward by the yeoman. Callie was pale as she took the chair, but her hands appeared relaxed in the lap of her white, spotless uniform.

"Lieutenant Donovan, please tell the board what happened a week ago at the O Club beginning at approximately 1900."

Swallowing hard, working to keep her voice calm and authoritative, Callie launched into the events. Luckily, she had a nearly photographic memory. What she couldn't remember, she had jotted down on small index cards. Ty had stressed that she should remember as clearly as possible the actual words said by the pilots and herself.

She felt sweat running from beneath her arms and trickling down the sides of her rib cage. When Ty moved to one side, she saw all three pilots glaring at her nonstop. Fear jagged through her, and for an instant, she lost her train of thought.

"Yes, Lieutenant?"

Ty's unruffled voice cut through her terror. Callie went on, reciting the events that had taken place in the O Club itself, and then out in the parking lot. The strain was terrible, because not once did the pilots stop looking at her, accusation, disrespect and anger in their eyes. If not for Ty's calming presence, his occasional question to prompt her memory, she was sure she couldn't have gotten through the narration.

By the time she got to the attack, her voice was quavering, and she couldn't help it. She couldn't keep the feelings or the terror at bay. Gripping the arms of the chair, she closed her eyes and saw the horrifying scene all over again. Slowly, carefully, she recounted everything. Everything. Her uniform was soaked with perspiration by the time she finished. Her heart was pounding hard in her chest, and she felt as if she might suffocate, needing badly to draw some fresh air into her lungs.

The pilots now wore expressions of overt hatred on their faces and Callie gulped convulsively. She glanced up at the board and found no sign of emotion, much less compassion. A cold chill worked its way through her, and she sat in the chair, feeling like a butterfly pinned to a board to die.

"I suggest," Ty told the board, "that it's fifteen minutes until lunch."

"We're in recess until 1400," the Commander said with a stroke of his gavel.

The board rose and everyone leaped to attention, including Callie. She barely caught herself—her knees were so weak that if she hadn't locked them, she'd have fallen on her nose. The commanders left the room first, followed by the pilots and their counsels. She saw Dr. Johnson get up and smile broadly at her. At the same moment, she felt Ty's hand come to rest on the small of her back.

"You were terrific," he whispered proudly.

"Wonderful!" Dr. Johnson agreed enthusiastically, coming up and hugging her effusively. "What a *great* witness you were! Not only were you clear and concise, but you conveyed just the right amount of emotion."

Callie sank against Ty momentarily. All she wanted was to be held. But that couldn't be, and she knew it. They were in a military situation and fraternizing wasn't allowed. She moved away from Ty, but gave him a silent look of thanks for being there.

"I don't know about the right amount of feeling," Callie said, grateful for the doctor's support. "I felt like my voice was shaking in my throat toward the end of the recall."

"Anyone who was attacked the way you were would have the very same feelings and emotions," Dr. Johnson soothed. She patted Callie on the shoulder and looked at Ty. "Commander, will you need me this afternoon?"

"Yes. Any one of those three counsels can call you back to the chair for questioning."

Callie walked between them as they left the warm, stuffy room that had so little natural light in it. "They'll ask you questions, Dr. Johnson, and they'll run their swords through me."

Ty said nothing, but he knew Callie wasn't wrong. He'd been aware of the level of malevolence in the pilots' faces during Callie's recounting of the incident. Feeling helpless as never before, he knew there was very little he could do to protect her once the counsels started trying to pick her story apart and making her appear to be a fool, or worse, a liar.

Chapter Ten

"Lieutenant Donovan, what were you doing at the Officer's Club that night at 1900?" Jason Lewis asked smoothly as he moved toward the chair where Callie sat. He straightened the sleeve of his gray, eight-hundred-dollar, Italian silk suit and gave her a brief, perfunctory smile before turning around and giving the board a deferential nod, acknowledging their power over the proceedings.

Callie forced her emotions, her fear, into a place deep within herself. She knew that above all, Lewis was going to try to poke holes into the truth of what had happened—to make Remington look like the victim instead of the harasser. She looked up at the small, solid man. His bulldog-type face was complete with jowls. Obviously Lewis was getting wealthy practicing law in the civilian world, the extra flesh testament to the good life.

"As I said in my opening remarks, I was getting a quick meal before heading over to the college to teach my photography class."

"Couldn't you have gone to any junk-food drive-in just as easily?" he offered.

Callie hated the way Lewis was smiling—as if he were about to stab her. "The O Club was the closest," she said.

"Or perhaps you knew that Commander Remington would be there?" he suggested, his voice silky.

Surprised, Callie felt her mouth drop open. "I beg your pardon?"

"Commander Remington always goes to the O Club after work to share a few beers with the boys, Lieutenant. Everyone knows that."

Callie saw where Lewis was trying to lead her, and she shrugged. "Mr. Lewis, I resent the fact that you're trying to make it look as if I deliberately went to the O Club to see Commander Remington. Nothing could be further from the truth. I spend eight to twelve hours a day, five days a week with him, and I certainly don't wish to extend it beyond that."

Raising his thin eyebrows, Lewis smiled deeply. "From what I understand, you've been chasing Commander Remington from the day you arrived here, Lieutenant Donovan."

Callie stared at the attorney and was about to retort when she heard Ty's voice.

"Mr. Lewis, I suggest you get away from innuendos and conjectures and stick to the facts about the night Lieutenant Donovan was attacked and assaulted by your client."

Lewis dropped his smile for just a moment, glaring in Ty's direction. He glanced over his shoulder at the board, and Commander Newton nodded his agreement.

"Of course," he murmured smoothly, and smiled down at Callie, the seed successfully planted in the minds of the men on the board anyway. "What were you wearing to the O Club on the night in question—whatever your reason for being there?"

Callie hated the implication from Lewis. "I wore a simple white blouse, a denim skirt and sandals."

"How provocative was the blouse, Lieutenant? How many buttons were unbuttoned? Did the blouse opening reveal the cleft of your breasts to anyone? Was it a transparent, see-through kind of material?"

Callic gasped. Before she could answer, Ty was again standing up.

"Mr. Lewis, I don't really think you're interested in what Lieutenant Donovan was wearing as much as in trying to establish in the board's mind something else—to paint her as provocative or a tease. Will you please ask only one question at a time and wait to hear my client's answers?"

Lewis rubbed his hands together and saw the board agree with Ballard. "Very well, Lieutenant, let's go back to my original question. How provocative was the blouse you were wearing?"

Angry, Callie said, "It was a plain white blouse, Mr. Lewis."

"Transparent in any way?"

"Of course not! It was 100 percent cotton and completely opaque."

"Did it button down the front?"

"Yes."

"How many buttons were buttoned?"

"All of them," Callie grated.

"I see.... And the skirt, Lieutenant. How short was your skirt? You know, nowadays, miniskirts are in again."

Holding on to her disintegrating temper, Callie realized she had to stop rising to Lewis's bait. His job was to stir her up, get her angry and make her look to the board like a hysterical woman. "My denim skirt, which, by the way, is opaque and not transparent, falls halfway down my calves. It's called a ballet-length skirt, Mr. Lewis, showing only my ankles."

"I see." He smiled. "And your sandals? Were they open-toed?"

"What pair of sandals isn't?" Callie shot back coolly.

"Were your toenails painted?"

At a loss, Callie stared at him. "Excuse me?"

"Were your toenails painted? For instance, a bright red color?"

"No."

"What about your fingernails?"

"Mr. Lewis, I don't wear any kind of makeup. Is that clear?"

"Perfume?" He lifted his nose and inhaled. "I can certainly smell that tantalizing, come-hither perfume you're wearing, Lieutenant. Did you wear perfume the night in question?"

Callie chafed under Lewis's implication that wearing any kind of nail polish, makeup or perfume would be signaling Remington that she was available for the kind of unwanted attention he gave her. That was what Lewis was trying to establish in the minds of the board. "I always wear a dab of perfume."

"Perfume is very much a sexual signal, you know, Lieutenant Donovan," he said silkily, smiling at the row of commanders. "It's like a subtle indicator to men—a nonverbal message that you're interested in them."

"Objection!" Ty said, standing again. He nailed Lewis with a dark look. "I hope the board doesn't buy into Mr. Lewis's unqualified opinion about a woman wearing perfume. I will point out that Dr. Johnson can testify that harassers attack their targets regardless of what makeup or perfume the target is wearing. A woman should be allowed to dress any way she wants and not expect to be assaulted or harassed for it, any more than a man is for his choice of dress."

Callie silently applauded Ty's riposte to Lewis. She saw the lawyer scowl for just a moment, then, just as quickly, saw him smile again.

"Objection noted," Commander Nelson said. "Mr. Lewis, proceed."

"Of course. Now, Lieutenant, isn't it true that you asked for a table close to the open bar area, where you knew Commander Remington and his friends were drinking?"

"Absolutely not. I had no idea he was in the club."

"And that when you sat down, you were constantly looking toward the bar, searching for Commander Remington among the crowds of pilots?"

"No," Callie exclaimed, her hands tightening in anger. Her heart was beginning a slow pounding. She could feel Lewis mentally stalking her, trying to make her look like something she had never been.

"And that once you spotted Commander Remington, you kept smiling at him, giving him long, significant glances that made him think you wanted him to come over to your table and visit with you?"

"Absolutely not! As a matter of fact, I was eating when I happened to glance up in that direction and saw a number of pilots pointing at me and talking about me. I suspected they were discussing the article that had come out in the previous Sunday's newspaper. I did not realize Commander Remington was at the bar until he showed up at my table." She glared at Lewis. "Unannounced and uninvited, I might add. I, in no way, wanted him near me in any sense of the word."

"Now, Lieutenant Donovan," Lewis said expansively, gesturing toward the row of pilots staring at her, "I have four witnesses who swear you were not only batting your eyelashes at Commander Remington, giving him come-hither glances, but had actually raised your hand and gestured for him to come over to your table. All four pilots saw you blow him a kiss while he stood at the bar."

Outraged, Callie nearly leaped out of the chair. She gripped the armrest, her fingers digging into the wood. No! Terror gripped her as she realized that not only were the three pilots who'd sexually harassed her involved with such a blatant lie, but Lieutenant Clark, the pilot who had sat two tables away, was also going to lie to make her look as if she had asked for Remington's advances.

For long seconds Callie sat tensely, trying to control her shock and fury. Lewis stood there smiling, looking impeccably cool and collected. She sat back, terror deluging her in a new way. If the board believed the four pilots' concocted story, she would be found to be to blame, and it would be her career that would suffer cruelly from those lies. Never had Callie dreamed that the pilots might lie to such an extent. But then, at Annapolis, she'd seen the upperclassmen close ranks on her in a similar manner. Why should she expect this to be different?

"Mr. Lewis," Callie rasped, her voice clear and carrying through the room with chilling authority, "I don't care what made-up stories you've been fed by those three pilots, or by Lieutenant Clark. I at no time invited Commander Remington over to my table with a look or a gesture. I never even had eye contact with him."

"As a matter of fact," Lewis boomed, "when Commander Remington came over to your table, and you made a suggestive comment about your legs being even prettier than his wife's—"

"That's a lie! Commander Remington made a rude remark about *my* legs, Mr. Lewis. I tried to defuse his unwanted advance by saying that I was sure his wife had very nice legs, too."

"—And you told Commander Remington that you'd like him and his two friends to escort you to your car after you'd eaten. Now," Lewis purred, looking at the board significantly, "I don't exactly call that minding your own business, Lieutenant Donovan. I call that being a tease. I call that asking for it."

"Objection!" Ty thundered. He moved away from his chair and toward the center of the room, behind where Callie sat. "Mr. Lewis is conjecturing and putting words in the mouth of my client. He has again both asked the questions and answered them for her."

"Agreed," the leader of the tribunal said. "Sit down, Commander Ballard."

Callie began to sweat in earnest now. She saw exactly how Lewis was going to paint her: she was a tease, she'd asked for Remington's advances, and in the parking lot, when she'd decided not to 'put out,' she'd pushed them away.

Rubbing his hands together, Lewis slowly turned to her. "The way you walked through the parking lot was provocative, Lieutenant."

"Mr. Lewis, a woman has a different walk than a man. I walked my usual walk. If you want to say it was provocative, then that's your opinion."

"That's my client's opinion," Lewis said. "You were *really* swaying your hips, Lieutenant." He used his hands to show the amount of exaggerated movement. "It was very pronounced swaying, Lieutenant, and Commander Remington and his friends saw it for what it was."

"Really?" Callie demanded scathingly, glaring at the row of pilots. The lying bastards. "Why is it I'm the one who was attacked, humiliated and assaulted, and these officers and supposed gentlemen are crying foul over the way I walked?"

Lewis frowned and took a step back. "That's not the way they see it, Lieutenant."

"I can tell," Callie snarled. "I didn't ask for Commander Remington's touches, nor did I ever agree to his innuendos about me, about my body. He made me terribly uncomfortable, and all I wanted to do was escape from the O Club and get out of his line of fire."

"I see," Lewis murmured. "Then would you like to tell the Board why it was you who reached out and touched Commander Remington's neck, shoulder and arm with your hand?"

Gasping, Callie sat there in shock. Remington, who had done that exact thing to her in the parking lot, was simply turning everything around to make it look as if she were the aggressor, not him. "He touched *me!* I never touched him except to push him and those two other officers away from me!''

''Now, Lieutenant. The way I understand it, you not only caressed Commander Remington in a number of ways, but you placed his hand across your shoulders and pressed it to the side of your breast.''

Callie sat very still, allowing the silence to fall over the room. She locked eyes with Remington, who was barely smiling, his green eyes glittering, and she felt hatred. Lewis was standing beside her, rocking heel to toe in his expensive black Italian leather shoes. The shattering reality of what was going to happen filled her with nausea. It would be four pilots' words against her own.

''Well?'' Lewis goaded. ''Answer the question, Lieutenant.''

Jerking a look up at the lawyer, Callie whispered, ''I never invited Remington's touch. I did not put his arm around my shoulders. I never pressed his hand to the side of my breast.''

''I suppose you're going to tell me that you didn't throw yourself bodily at Lieutenant Dale Oakley?''

''No,'' Callie said with gritted teeth. ''When Commander Remington threw his arm around me and started to touch my breast, I pushed him away. In doing so, I fell off balance and slammed into Lieutenant Oakley. He then threw his arms around me and tried to kiss me. I yelled, 'Stop,' but he wouldn't listen. So I pushed him away and fell back against my car.''

''Lieutenant Thorson was your next target, and you moved provocatively into his arms and told him you were known as the Ice Queen, right? Didn't you say that you liked the fact he had a Corvette and Armani suits, and that you liked his style?''

"Nothing could be further from the truth, Mr. Lewis, and I don't see how you can stand there and defend such lies."

"Will you kindly tell us your side of it?"

"Lieutenant Thorson reached out and grabbed me as I spun out of Lieutenant Oakley's grip. He grabbed me and said, 'Hey, look at this, guys—Ms. Ice Queen has fallen into my arms!' " Callie felt desperate. Her mind spun, looking for options, but there were none. She realized in despair that Ty Ballard could only do so much. For the next hour, she sweated out Lewis's questions. Finally, he was finished.

As Callie sat in the chair waiting for Lieutenant Oakley's counsel, a lieutenant commander, to come and begin cross-examining her, she wanted to run. There was no place to hide. There was no safety in any sense of the word. Trying to gather her strewn composure to deal with the next broadside fusillade to be leveled at her by Oakley's counsel, Callie wished that 1700 would arrive. That was the time the board would halt questioning, until 0900 the next morning.

Ty could hardly wait for Commander Newton to close the hearing for the day. Callie sat pale and tense in the chair as the third counsel for the pilots finished questioning her. Her lips were compressed, and her hands remained in a knot on her lap. He could see the sheen of perspiration on her face and felt a mixture of anger and anguish. After everyone came to attention, Ty moved to where Callie sat. He placed his hand on her shoulder to signal that she was to remain sitting until the room emptied. Dr. Johnson also stood quietly beside her.

When the pilots and their counsels had left, he touched her elbow and met her weary gaze. "Can you stand?"

Just the touch of Ty's hand sent a wave of stabilizing strength through her, and she managed a twist of her lips. "I don't know how—I've been shot at and hit so many times, a corpse would feel better than I do."

Ty grinned a little, sympathy in his eyes, and helped her stand. He forced himself to release her elbow and she slowly straightened and smoothed her wrinkled skirt. Marlene Johnson gently touched her shoulder.

"You did beautifully under the circumstances," she said. "It's not at all uncommon for counsels to take the position they did with you."

"They twisted everything around," Callie said, holding the psychiatrist's compassionate gaze. "Everything. It just blew me away. I wasn't expecting it."

"You were expecting them to stay at least within the general realm of the truth," Ty said. "And frankly, so was I."

Dr. Johnson shook her head. "No, that's not the way it works, Commander Ballard. I tried to warn you about such tactics several days ago when you came to my office."

Angry with himself because he hadn't listened to her he muttered, "I'm sorry I didn't." Giving Callie an apologetic look, Ty felt as if he'd abandoned her in some important way.

"Even if you had believed Dr. Johnson," Callie said softly, moving and stretching her tense, aching muscles, "it wouldn't have done any good."

"Maybe not," Ty said unhappily.

"I think," Dr. Johnson said, "that what you two need is a good meal in a private, quiet spot. Let down, relax, and then talk about tomorrow's maneuvers. Commander, it will be up to you to try to force these four pilots into slipping up and mixing their story lines. Somehow, you have to create doubt in the mind of the board, or they will definitely buy their story and Callie's career will be destroyed.''

Glumly, Callie agreed. She stood next to Ty, adding her profound thanks to his as Dr. Johnson said good-night and left, agreeing to be back the next morning. The room was barren and silent. Callie glanced up, to find Ty's face looking set and hard.

"I feel for you," she murmured. "This isn't going to look good for your career, either. Lewis is a pro at this. He's impressing the board no matter what you try to do."

With a nod, Ty touched her elbow. "I don't regret being your counsel, Callie. I never will. We know the truth, and that's what matters. Remember, my report is in the board's hands, too. I saw it happening. They may want to discount your version because you're a woman, but they can't as easily discount mine, so don't give up yet."

Callie walked slowly out of the room with him. She desperately wanted to escape the suffocating climate the room symbolized.

"We're lucky," Ty said. "Since this hearing is being held on station, the press can't get to us." The passageway was devoid of people, narrow and silent. "Right now we could be swamped with cameras, lights and microphones stuck in our faces."

"I guess there is some good news," Callie said glumly.

He smiled slightly and pulled her to a halt. Making sure there were no prying eyes, he touched her arm.

"I'll follow you back to your apartment, and I want you to get into some comfortable old clothes."

Puzzled, Callie searched his face, which suddenly looked less harsh. Looking into his eyes, which sparkled with intent, she asked, "Why?"

"Because," Ty said, "I'm taking you to the ocean, to walk on the beach. We'll stop at a delicatessen on the way and grab something to eat. A beach picnic. I think that's what you need, and so do I."

Grateful for his care, his insight into her emotional state, which was completely frayed, Callie managed a soft, hesitant smile. "You really are a breed apart from most of these pilots."

Relieved that Callie was going along with his impromptu plan, Ty led her out of the Operations building and to the parking lot. Heat rolled in unrelenting waves across the black asphalt, while the sun hung low on the horizon.

"Don't judge all pilots by these four," he warned her. "Most aren't like Remington. Oh, we may be ignorant about what sexual harassment is really all about, but once we learn what it is, Callie, we aren't going to continue our practices. Believe me."

As Ty opened the door of her car for her, Callie did believe that most of the navy pilots weren't like Remington; she'd just had the bad luck of getting saddled with him at her job—and stuck in a situation where she had no choice but to fight back. As she leaned against the hot upholstery before starting the engine, she closed her eyes and allowed another layer of tension to dissolve. The ocean. How badly she needed to be there right now. Surprisingly, despite the trauma and tension of the day, Callie was looking forward to sharing it with Ty.

"I'm so glad you thought of this," Callie said as she sat cross-legged on a dark blue cotton blanket. Across from her, Ty, dressed in a white polo shirt and tan shorts, lay on his side, propped up on one elbow, eating heartily from the variety of food that sat between them. If possible, he looked even more appealing because he was barefoot, his feet large and wide, dark hair covering his calves and well-formed thighs. A boyish quality had replaced today's hard, eaglelike demeanor. Callie wondered if this was the real Ty Ballard—the man who seemed at ease next to the ocean enjoying the call of the sea gulls, the crash of the surf and reveling in the aura of peace.

"I'm glad I thought of it, too. It's relaxing out here." And they were alone. Most of the tourists were gone, since the sun was beginning to set. Ty reached for another sweet pickle and crunched it contentedly. The last hour had been bliss, in his opinion, although he didn't share that thought with Callie. She sat facing the ocean, her legs drawn up. Wearing a loose, sleeveless plaid blouse and a pair of obviously old, tattered slacks that were frayed just below her knees, she presented a picture of tranquility to him. The soft, intermittent sea breeze ruffled her black hair and gave her a childlike look. Nowhere to be found was the navy officer who had graduated from Annapolis, and Ty was stunned by the change that the ocean brought in her.

Callie nibbled at the beef sandwich on sourdough bread, not really tasting it. She knew she had to eat to keep up her strength, that "round two" tomorrow morning would continue to shred her good name and career. Ty, on the other hand, was starved, and made no apologies for the fact he'd consumed two huge beef sandwiches, most of the sweet pickles and over half the potato salad. The bottle of wine was half-empty, and Callie picked up her plastic cup and sipped a little more of the rosé liquid.

"There's something healing about the ocean," she murmured, holding the cup in front of her legs. Resting her chin on her drawn-up knees, Callie added, "Wouldn't it be nice if we could take this feeling that exists here back with us to that hearing? There wouldn't be any lies, any negativity."

Ty sat up and poured more wine into his cup. Callie's voice was roughened with emotion, with a kind of hope that he knew didn't exist for her in that hearing room. He ached to reach over and caress her pale cheek, smooth the tautness from her skin and take the darkness from her sad eyes.

"I know this is going to sound stupid," he said, holding her gaze, "but while you were being savaged by Lewis, all I wanted to do was jump up, punch the guy out and then make my way down the line, starting with Remington, and beating the hell out of each of them until they told the real truth of what happened."

A warmth touched Callie, and she drowned in the dark gray of Ty's gaze. His voice was low, vibrating with feeling, and it made her feel better. For the hundredth time, Callie wanted to allow Ty to hold her, and yes, to kiss her again. His mouth was wonderfully shaped, the corners turning up a bit, giving him an impish quality. Ty had the ability to laugh, and that was something she felt was important. He also could laugh at himself. His ego was not as inflated as those of other pilots she'd known.

"The knight riding to rescue the damsel?" she teased.

"Something like that." He sighed. "I guess old ways, ingrained habits, die hard, Callie. I found myself angrier than I've ever been in there today."

"This isn't a hearing, it's an inquisition," she said. "I'm a modern-day witch to be burned at the stake in the name of maintaining male dominance. This isn't about finding the truth, it's about covering up so that men don't have to pay for their behavior. Boys will be boys."

"I can't disagree," he murmured. "And I've got to tell you, I'm ashamed of what's going on in there. I'm stunned that Remington would lie. That these pilots, who are supposed to be leaders showing the way to our enlisted people, are setting such a bad example." With a shake of his head, he added, "I just wouldn't have believed this unless I was there to see it."

"I know," Callie said softly, "that a lot of guys don't understand what their sexual harassment does to us, Ty. It's terrible. If they'd just ask one simple question before they did it, I think it would solve a lot of problems."

"What question is that?" He took a sip of the wine, noticing how the pale gold of the sunset mirrored Callie's beauty.

"Would they say or do the same thing to their sister, their wife or their daughter?"

"Good point. I see what you mean."

"And if they wouldn't, then they shouldn't be doing it or saying it at all."

Much later, Ty opened the door to her apartment for Callie. He didn't want to leave, but knew he must.

The shadowed look on Callie's face convinced him she felt similarly. All evening he'd ached to hold her and kiss her. There was no one around the apartment, and Ty reached out and placed his hand on her upper arm.

"Come here," he whispered, and gently pulled Callie toward him.

Her breath hitching, Callie moved into Ty's embrace. Just the tenderness burning in his eyes made her forget everything—if only for a moment. How badly she had wanted this, wanted him. As he lifted his hand and caressed her cheek, she closed her eyes and pressed against his palm. A sigh escaped her as his arm tightened around her. His body was lean and strong. It was so easy to surrender to Ty's touch, to his whispered words that spilled out near her ear.

"I want you," he rasped, as he felt her arms move around his waist. "Just as day wants night, and the ocean needs the sands to race up on...."

Callie lifted her head and tilted it upward just in time to feel his mouth mold hotly against her own. The scent of Ty, his maleness, his tenderness as his mouth slid across hers, all combined to loosen her hold on reality. The board hearing no longer existed. Her career hanging in the balance no longer mattered. Just the hungry questing of his mouth against hers, his ragged breathing were important, and need thrummed through her.

Moments stolen out of time grew molten as she felt his fingers move languidly against her arched spine, and a moan came from deep within her. He was strong, sure, yet sensitive to her as he monitored the amount of pressure he placed against her soft, opened mouth. As the tip of his tongue slid tantalizingly across her lower lip, Callie felt the world start to tilt wildly out of balance. She was no longer thinking. She was just intensely feeling each of his caresses, his hungry, searching kisses and the sensation that she was, indeed, well loved.

Dazed, Callie pulled away and looked up at Ty's dark face. Night had fallen and the streetlight to the left made his expression look like that of an eagle that had spotted its prey. But she felt anything but threatened in his arms, beneath his melting kisses and evocative touches. Her body vibrated with heat, color and rampant need. Never had anyone made her feel like this, and she sucked in a ragged breath.

"Take it easy," he said thickly, easing Callie into the foyer and nudging the door closed with his heel. Ty didn't want to let her go. He wanted to love her completely. The luster in Callie's blue eyes was touched with desire. Her lips were parted, moist and begging to be ravished again. His body throbbed restlessly beneath his steel control, and it took every ounce of Ty's inner strength not to pick Callie up and carry her to her bedroom.

The moments glided and dissolved together for Callie as she remained in Ty's embrace. The gray of his eyes reminded her of a turbulent storm, and she, too, felt chaotic inside, her needs clashing with the pressures closing in around them. Where had the idea of being well loved come from? Tilting her head, she absorbed Ty's hungry look. Could it be? But how? Callie had no answers, and she felt cheated by time, which wasn't on their side.

"I should go," Ty rasped with a sliver of a one-cornered smile, "but it's the last thing I want to do, Callie. The last."

She nodded faintly. Never had she wanted a man more than him, intuitively realizing that he wasn't like the men of her past, but very different. "I—I know."

"You feel the same way?" He didn't dare believe Callie felt as deeply for him as he did about her. Yet, as she lifted those thick, black lashes and looked up at him, Ty felt his breath being torn from him.

"It's so soon," she whispered unsteadily. "I mean—" she avoided the burning look in his eyes "—I don't normally fall like this...."

Ty's heart soared and he felt as if his life had finally—after more than a year of penance—been handed back to him. He framed Callie's face, poignantly aware of the tears in her eyes. "I know you don't," he said raggedly. "But I don't care, sweetheart. I do care for you, for what you want of me. All you have to do is say the word, Callie. I won't push you. I can't." Above all, Ty recognized that something in her past would never allow him to push her beyond the pace she set for them. Grateful that she longed for him as much as he did for her, an odd contentment spread through him. This was the sweetest wait that he would ever undertake. To have Callie come to him, walk into his arms and share herself with him in every way was a dream he'd never dared dream.

Reaching up, Callie touched Ty's jaw. She felt the prickly beard beneath her palm and smiled softly. "It's all so crazy."

"Yes, everything is crazy."

"Maybe it's the situation," Callie ventured as she allowed herself to explore his jaw and cheek. The burning light in Ty's eyes made her feel bold in a new and exciting way. Each time she caressed his skin, she felt him tremble against her, reminding her of a race horse straining to run.

Ty shook his head and captured her hand. He kissed it. "The situation brought us together," he said, "and if anything, I think it's slowed down what would have happened if things were different."

Callie couldn't argue with Ty's insight. "From the moment I saw you in the parking lot, I knew I'd be safe," she admitted. "It was you. The look in your eyes."

With a careless smile, Ty said, "Sweetheart, you hit me over the head with your beauty."

Callie had never thought of herself as beautiful, but the way Ty said it made her believe he really saw her as that—and more. Heat rushed up her neck and into her face. The smile on Ty's mouth translated to his eyes and she knew he liked her blush. As if reading her intentions, he slowly released her.

"Maybe when this board thing is over, we can get on with our lives," Ty said, hope in his voice. "Would you like that?" Never had he wanted her to say yes more than now.

Smoothing her hair across her brow, she said, "I think I'd like that."

"We need time," Ty agreed. "And space."

Callie understood at that moment just how much the board hearing had impinged upon their burgeoning relationship. "But if it hadn't happened, we'd never have met."

"That's true," Ty said. He reached over and gripped her hand. "Try and get a good night's sleep tonight, all right?"

Shakily, Callie nodded, unable to slake the hunger that prowled through her for Ty. All she had to do was look at his very male mouth, the way it curved so confidently at the corners, and she went hot with need all over again. "Yes . . . I'll try. . . ."

Chapter Eleven

"Commander Remington," Ty began, "would you describe the philosophy you have toward women to the board?" He stood off to one side, his hands behind his back. Remington had just finished telling his version of what had happened, and it was Ty's turn to cross-examine him. As expected, Remington had lied about everything, turning around what he'd done to Callie to make the board believe she had led him on instead. Out of the corner of his eye, he saw Callie sitting against the wall, Dr. Johnson next to her. He was glad they'd had the opportunity to go to the ocean last night, because it had helped shore up Callie emotionally. Ty had wanted to spend longer at the beach, and he'd wanted to become more intimate with her after those burning kisses, but it wasn't the right time. He'd spent the rest of the night, until about 0300, creating questions designed to show the board Remington's real attitude toward women.

Remington leaned back and crossed his legs nonchalantly. "I like them."

The pilots snickered, and two of the board members smiled. Ty glared at the tribunal and then at the pilots. Instantly, two of the three members on the board stopped smiling, their faces falling somber again. It was a telling reaction and his heart sank.

"Can you be more specific?"

With an expansive shrug, Remington said, "I'm a man, and a woman's a woman. I'm strong and powerful—women are beautiful and sexy."

"What do you mean by powerful?"

"I'm stronger."

"Stronger in a physical sense or in being able to dominate them?"

"Both."

"You believe men should dominate women?"

"They have since caveman days. What's so different now?"

Ty glanced up to see Callie's expression, which was one of utter fury. He saw the board's reaction, too: one of silent agreement with Remington's views.

"How do you see yourself as a man?"

"I'm a fighter pilot. A Top Gun. I'm the best there is."

"And before you were married, how did you see yourself in relation to the women you liked?"

Remington smiled a little, a gloating smile. "Listen, it was open season. I was the hunter, they were the quarry. They're to be enjoyed. If I set my gun sites on one, I chased her until I caught her. She was mine, and she knew it. I scored on her."

"How did you do this?"

Remington laughed. "Now, Commander, I wouldn't want to give away any of my trade secrets to you."

The polite laughter that followed made Ty's blood boil. Remington was enjoying this line of questioning, not realizing how it made him out to be a harasser. "Humor me," Ty said, "and try."

"Fine. I never had fewer than ten women at any time who wanted me. They liked sex and so did I. There are a lot of pilots who are jealous of my ability to pick up the groupies at the bar, but I do something they don't."

"And that is?"

"Most of the pilots can't even get a woman to talk to them. I just march right up and show them how it's done."

"How is it 'done?' "

"I throw my arm around her, bring her up against me, smile a big smile that tells her I want her body and I ask her for a date. A real man doesn't mess around. He gets straight to the point, if you know what I mean." Remington smiled hugely at his fellow pilots, who were all grinning like a cheerleading section.

"So, you hustle a woman?"

"Call it what you want. I know how to move into their territory and stake my claim on 'em."

"What if the woman doesn't want your kind of attention?"

"No woman can resist my tactics."

"But if she did?"

Remington scowled. "I told you—I always score."

"You ever get physical with your ladies?"

"My women enjoy having sex with me, and if it gets a little rough, they like it that way. They like being tamed. It's part of the old psychology of 'me caveman, you woman,' you know?"

"I see." Ty brought out several documents and walked over to the board, placing them before the officers to view. "I'd like to submit for the record a document that I got from the legal department. Six months ago, Commander Remington was charged with assault on a civilian woman called Cindy Laker." Ty looked grimly at Remington, whose mouth had dropped opened, and then up at the board members, who were studying the copies. "Cindy Laker was eighteen years old and had come to the O Club with a friend who was twenty. What the board should know—"

"Objection!" Lewis said. "This hearing is about the incident that took place last week, not six months ago."

"On the contrary," Ty growled, "this document should be considered as evidence because it shows a past history of Commander Remington physically assaulting another woman in the same setting and circumstances."

Remington sat stiffly, suddenly alert, his eyes flashing with rage. "That chick deserved it! She was a tease! She flaunted herself at me and when I gave her the attention she wanted, she went whining and crying to the shore patrol."

Ty smiled a little as the board continued to read the charges. "The attention you gave her was similar to the attention you just gave Lieutenant Donovan, Commander."

Callie sat there, stunned. She hadn't realized Ty had carried out such a thorough investigation on her behalf. Tears flooded into her eyes as she began to understand how much Ty did care for her. She remained very still, absorbing the truth of him fully—for the first time totally separating him from her past negative experiences with pilots. In that moment, she saw him in an entirely different light. A kinder one, filled with promise and, for the first time in her life, a burning hope.

"That little bitch asked for it!" Remington thundered angrily, and he shook his index finger at Ty. "She wore this tight little leather miniskirt and see-through blouse. What was I to do? To think?"

"Again," Ty said in a stern voice, "a harasser sees an invitation no matter what a woman is wearing. In this country, a woman has the right to wear whatever she wants, and a man shouldn't automatically think she's a piece of meat up on the selling block, a sexual object to be 'owned' by some male." He moved quickly from the dais to stand behind Remington, who'd been glaring at him. "I want to tell the board what Dr. Johnson has found about sexual harassers and their psychological profiles. One type, known as the 'Gunfighter' personality, feels he's the ultimate macho man. He views women as a challenge to be met, overcome and conquered—whether she wants him or not. Further, this psychological profile thinks women are to be enjoyed and cannot see them as human beings, only as objects to be possessed by him. He's into power and control over a woman. He can talk about them only in sexual terminology because that's the only way he perceives them. He describes himself as 'a stud' or manly, and he is aggressive in his pursuit of his target.''

Ty turned and nailed Remington directly as he went on, his voice rolling through the room. ''A woman is seen as a score—nothing more. She isn't seen as a human being who has a heart, who has feelings, because this type of man invalidates her human qualities with his own projections of himself. He chases for the fever of the hunt. Once he 'catches' his quarry, he takes what he wants from her and walks away. That is the psychological profile on this kind of harasser. And I believe you can see by Commander Remington's own words—his view of himself and how he perceives women—that he fits this profile.''

Ty stood there savoring the small victory for Callie. He knew that at Lewis's objections, the board would throw out the document proving Remington had been charged with the assault of Cindy Laker. The charges had later been dropped because Cindy hadn't wanted to be put on the stand and grilled—just as Callie was now being grilled. Still, it allowed Ty to plant the seeds in the board's mind, and to give him the opportunity to use Dr. Johnson's considerable weight as an expert in the field to make them look differently at Remington—even if the four pilots continued to lie about the incident to protect themselves and their careers.

As he waited, he glanced in Callie's direction. He saw such hope in her face that his heart raced momentarily. There were tears in her blue eyes, too, but not out of sorrow. Ty literally felt her admiration for him, felt the feelings she'd been hiding from him and it left him reeling with discovery. For a brief moment, he smiled at her—a smile that said so much—man to woman, not counsel to client.

To Ty's disappointment, if not his surprise, the board did not accept the document into evidence. He saw Remington smile hugely, as if he'd won the round. Moving toward the pilot, Ty changed his line of questioning.

"Commander, are you married?"

"You know I am."

"How long have you been married?"

"Two years."

"First marriage?"

"No, my third."

"I see."

"Yours didn't stay together, either," Remington shot back.

Ty held on to his anger. "My marriage is not up for discussion at this hearing, Commander."

"Well, neither is mine."

"You're wrong," Ty breathed softly. "Tell me what your third wife is like, Commander."

Relaxing, Remington grinned. "She's a nice little woman. She stays home, fixes my meals and makes sure my needs are met."

"Does you present wife hold an outside job?"

"Hell, no!"

"Why not?"

"I won't let her, that's why. I damn well make enough money that she doesn't have to go galavanting off and be like all the rest of these women."

"What do you mean by that comment, Commander?"

Remington snorted. "There isn't a man alive who likes feminists. They're a bunch of dykes wanting to control us men, that's all."

"I believe," Ty said mildly, "that when Lieutenant Donovan pushed you away and told you she didn't want your advances, you called her a lesbian."

Flashing a look of hatred, Remington snarled, "Most of the women in the military are lesbian."

"Perhaps just the ones that say no to your advances?"

"Look," Remington growled, "these women think they can replace us men in the navy. Well, they're wrong! They aren't strong enough physically, and they ain't got the brains it takes. I don't have a problem with enlisted women, they're the same as the enlisted men, but I don't like women officers who think they're as good as I am, because they aren't."

"Commander, I'm sure you're aware that the navy doesn't tolerate homosexuals. So, are you charging Lieutenant Donovan?" Ty smiled to himself, knowing he'd caught Remington.

"Of course not!"

"But you accused her of being a dyke and a lesbian."

"I did not!"

"Then Lieutenant Donovan is lying again, and you're telling the truth?"

Breathing hard, Remington gripped the arms of the chairs. "Yes!"

Satisfied that the pilot had placed doubt on his testimony, Ty didn't pursue it. "I have no more questions. You may step down, Commander Remington."

Lieutenant Neil Thorson came to the stand. Ty sat next to Callic making notes about his testimony—

which paralleled Remington's perfectly. When it was his turn to cross-examine, he glanced at Callie. He could see the tension in her face and the darkness in her eyes. Giving her a slight smile, he rose, legal pad in hand as he made his way to where Thorson sat.

"Lieutenant Thorson, are you married?"

"Yes, I am."

Ty nodded. The black-haired pilot was lean, his eyes snapping with alertness. "Had you met Lieutenant Donovan before the night of the incident?"

Thorson smiled over at the cadre of pilots before answering. "Let's put it this way, Commander—Ms. Donovan's reputation preceded her to the station."

Frowning, Ty felt uneasy. He saw a glitter in Thorson's eyes that he didn't like. Had Lewis or one of the other counsels uncovered something from Callie's past?

"Would you care to elaborate?" Ty demanded.

"Be glad to. I have a friend, Lieutenant Jerry Ivers—"

Ty heard Callie gasp and snapped his head in her direction. He saw her start to launch herself out of the chair. Holding up his hand in a silent plea for her to sit down and remain quiet, he zeroed in on Thorson. "Go on."

"Ivers went through Annapolis with her," Thorson said, savoring every word as if it were dessert, "and he told me about her reputation of being a big-time tease to her fellow plebes."

"That's a lie!" Callie cried, coming to her feet. Fists knotted at her side, she said, "A lie!"

Ty winced outwardly at her cry of absolute pain riddled with fury. Instantly, he turned to the board. "I request a thirty-minute recess to confer with my client."

Commander Newton nodded. "A thirty-minute recess," he boomed, striking the gavel.

Without a word, Ty turned on his heel, gripped Callie by the elbow and guided her out of the room. There was an office across the passageway and he took her in there. Shutting the door, he stood near it and watched her contorted features.

"What's going on?" he demanded. "Who's Ivers?"

Callie's hands were shaking as she brought them to her face. She tried to stop the scream that was unwinding deep in her gut, and she couldn't stop breathing in ragged gasps. Hearing Ty's voice, she was unable to respond. Tears flooded into her eyes.

Concerned, Ty moved to her side and gently placed his hands on her shoulders. She was trembling. "Callie? Please...what's going on? Talk to me."

Just the caress of his hands on her shoulders gave her the courage to lift her head and meet his stormy eyes. Tears coursed down her cheeks and she opened her mouth to speak, but only a croak came out.

"It's okay," he soothed thickly, and briefly touched her hair. Ty wanted so badly to continue to touch her, to help her, but they didn't have that kind of time. "Take it from the beginning," he told her. "What happened at Annapolis, Callie? Every time I've mentioned that word, I've seen you blanch."

Shutting her eyes and choking back a sob, she whispered brokenly, "Ivers hated me. He hated any woman who dared to think she could make it through the academy. He was an upperclassman, two years ahead of me. Wh-when I was a plebe in my first year, he and his gang started harassing me in every way possible." The pain rose as she relived the memories. Opening her eyes, she saw the blurred outline of Ty's grim features through her tears. His hands closed more firmly around her shoulders and she placed hers against his chest. The hardness in his face melted and she saw only worry and care there instead. It gave her the impetus to go on, no matter how humiliating, how shamed she felt.

"I—I tried to avoid Ivers and his gang of six friends, but it was impossible. Maggie was in her last year there, and Alanna was a year behind her. They couldn't help me—they didn't dare. There was such awful harassment toward us, Ty. The men hated us being there, and they showed it in so many ways. I felt cut off, helpless. Alanna and Maggie had warned me it would be tough, but I had no idea how bad it was going to be."

Ty nodded. He knew the first-year plebe at Annapolis took a horrendous amount of badgering from upperclassmen. He'd gone through that hellish first year himself, but he'd been a male, so he knew it hadn't been as hard as it had been on Callie and her sisters. "Okay, so far, so good. Ivers had it in for you."

"Y-yes. Oh, God, this is so hard to tell, Ty. I—I've never told anyone about it. Not even my sisters. Or," she added with a sob, "my folks—my mother...."

His gut twisting in pain for her, Ty gripped her by the shoulders. "You can tell me, Callie. I promise you, it's safe with me. If you don't, Lewis and those other counsels are going to use it against you in some way to sway the board's view of you. Come on, tell me the rest of it."

Taking a ragged breath, Callie stared up at him. The burning intensity of his eyes sent a ray of stability through her—enough, at least, to confide the rest of the incident. Her fingers dug briefly into the white cotton of his shirt and she felt the strength of his chest beneath it. Ty was so strong, so self-assured, when she felt none of those things. "One night at 0300, after I got off guard duty, I went back to my room at the dorm. My roommate had guard duty that shift and I was alone. Ivers and his gang burst through the door." Swallowing hard, Callie whispered, "None of the doors are ever locked, and they were supposed to knock and announce themselves, but they didn't." She bowed her head, ashamed. "They shut the door behind them, and they began to call me horrible names and push me around. They hated me because I was a woman on their male territory. That's what it boiled down to. They were intimidating me in every way to get me to quit the academy.

"I remember they got rougher with me. They formed a circle in the dorm room and started pushing me from one man to another. I tried to fight back, but it was impossible. I was so angry, and I was scared, too. At that time of morning, I knew no one would come to my defense. I got knocked to the floor a couple of times, and I kicked out at them." Miserably, Callie hung her head and added, "Finally, they left, and I remember sobbing as I made it to the door and shut it."

"My, God," Ty breathed, touching her cheeks with his hands, "did you report them? Did you tell your sisters?"

Choking on a sob, Callie said, "Report them? Seven of them against me? Who would the authorities believe? I was afraid to tell my sisters, because I knew both of them would move heaven and hell to get even with Ivers and his gang. If they did that, they'd both be kicked out, and I knew how much graduating and becoming navy officers meant to them. So I never told them. I sat on the floor, my back to the door, crying and shaking."

Cold-blooded anger moved through Ty. Without a word, he opened his arms and pulled Callie against him. He held her tightly, his head resting against her own as she began to weep in earnest. No safe place. There had never been a safe place for her. All thought of the board hearing melted away, and Ty focused on Callie's strength, her warmth. She had stood fast against such brutal treatment! Unconsciously, he rubbed her back with his hand and tried to soothe away some of her pain. Pressing against her hair small kisses meant to help, he inhaled her special feminine scent.

"It's going to be okay," he heard himself rasp. Would it be? No. Gently, he eased Callie away just enough to take his handkerchief and blot the tears from her face. She took the proffered cloth with a broken smile and dabbed her reddened eyes.

"I'm such a mess. The minute I go back in there, they'll know I've been crying."

"Let them," he growled. Caressing her hair, he said, "Callie, they're going to go after you on this. I'm going to have to tell them the truth. Otherwise, the board will accept the hearsay of Thorson. You know that, don't you?"

She stood there feeling utterly naked and gutted by a world that really didn't care that she had feelings, that she, ultimately, was a member of the human race.

Numbness swept through her. The stormy color of Ty's eyes told her so much that she reached out and touched his arm. There was such incredible tension within him, as if he were holding himself together so he wouldn't explode.

"Yes, I understand."

"I'm sorry...."

"You shouldn't be apologizing," she whispered, and handed him back the damp handkerchief.

He wanted to say more, but there was no time. "Tonight, after the hearing, I want you to come to my house. You need to be with someone for a little while. I don't want you to be alone right now."

Rallying beneath his quavering voice, Callie nodded. "Okay, but I'm not going to be very good company."

"I don't care." He gripped her arm. "Are you ready?"

"Yes."

From the patio of Ty's home, they watched the sun set behind a bank of gray stratus clouds that were working their way toward the coastline. Callie had eaten very little—some salad, a few bites of the steak that he'd fixed for her earlier. The glass of wine soothed some of her emotional distress, but not much. Ty was quieter than usual, too, but Callie understood. The afternoon session at the hearing had been barbaric. Lewis had gone on to paint her as a woman who'd had a reputation for teasing men from the time she'd entered Annapolis. To prove it, he'd provided an affidavit signed by Lieutenant Ivers, who was now stationed in Pensacola, Florida. The "good ol' boy" network was alive and well.

Ty came back out to the patio after loading the dirty dishes in the dishwasher. Dressed in a comfortable, dark blue short-sleeved shirt and chino pants, he met and held Callie's lifeless stare as he approached her lounge chair. She had changed into a pale pink sundress with a boat neck and white sandals. The picture of her was fetching—poignant.

"I can't believe you had twenty calls on your answering machine today," he said, sitting down next to her.

"I can't, either. I'll bet they're from more women who had suffered sexual harassment."

Ty nodded and sat on the edge of the chair, his hands clasped between his thighs. "I just never realized the extent of the problem," he murmured.

"You couldn't. You're not a woman."

He took her comment with good grace, because she'd not flung it at him in anger. It was merely a statement, a sad statement, of fact. Holding her gaze, he said, "I haven't done a very good job of defending you. I wish I could have done better, Callie." Tomorrow morning, the board would convene and announce their decision regarding the charges.

Reaching over, she touched his arm, aware of the warmth of his skin beneath her fingertips. "I think, for not being a lawyer, you've done an incredible job on my behalf. Don't be hard on yourself, Ty. I'm pleased. Isn't that all that counts?"

With a shake of his head, he captured her hand and brought it to his lips. "No," he whispered, "it's not," and he kissed the back of her fingers. Ty allowed her to reclaim her hand, but continued to hold her gaze, which spoke of desire along with grief and pain. "They're using you as a scapegoat. To put it in military lingo, they've gone beyond the line of departure with their dirty tricks and lies."

"Line of departure" was a military term referring to going beyond the point of no return. Remington and the other pilots, who, because they were Annapolis graduates, were supposed to honor the principles of truth and honesty, had veered away from that standard and lied. The regret in Ty's voice was echoed in his face.

"I'm ashamed to say I'm an Annapolis grad," he told her quietly. "Those men don't dignify the honor of what it's supposed to mean. Officers and gentlemen don't lie, they take it on the nose instead."

"You're an idealist," Callie said softly. "A white knight on a charger. Those days are gone, Ty. Truth, honor, dignity are parceled out by some men to others—but not across the board. There's a gender war going on out there. I just got caught up in it and so did you."

With a heavy shake of his head, he muttered, "I can't believe that the board will find them not guilty. My God, if they do..." He sat up, unable to comprehend such a decision.

"If they do, and I think they will," Callie said more strongly, "then it's the navy's way of sending the not-so-subtle message that zero tolerance against sexual harassment is a toothless tiger. A paper tiger, if you will. It looks and sounds good, and it's great PR for the civilian world, but in reality, there's nowhere for women in the service to get justice—to get the protection they deserve."

Ty suddenly stood up and he held out his hand to her. "Come on, let's go to the beach. I don't know how you feel, but I want to get away from this for a little while.''

Without hesitation, Callie reached out, curling her fingers into his strong ones, and allowed him to pull her to her feet. Without a word, still holding hands, they walked through the house to the car parked in the driveway.

A full moon was overhead, the Pacific Ocean smooth and glassy under its silvery radiance. The tide was out, and Callie walked slowly at Ty's side, her hand in his. They were both barefoot, the damp sand squishing between their toes, the foamy waters gurgling and playing tag with them as they made their way down the curved stretch of empty beach. The salt air was fragrant and slightly curled Callie's hair. The coolness was wonderful in comparison to Miramar's dry desert heat.

Tidal pools glowed like magical mirrors, and from time to time, Callie would lean down, her cotton dress gathering around her as she crouched to look at the moonlit beings who lived beneath the water. Ty would join her, his arm grazing her own and he would point to a slow-moving starfish, or they would appreciate the beauty of a flowerlike sea anemone that had opened its many tentacles to capture unseen plankton in the pool.

''When I was a kid,'' Ty told her in a low voice as they watched a starfish move slowly across one pool, ''I used to dream of seeing the ocean someday.''

''And what was your reaction when you did see it?'' Callie asked as she looked at his deeply shadowed features. There was such serenity and strength in his face.

Ty smiled at her. "The first time I saw it was when I visited the academy when I was seventeen. My parents took me to Chesapeake Bay and then over to the Atlantic Ocean on the other side. I was awed by the power of it, the beauty."

"I still am," Callie admitted softly.

Ty rose and brought her to her feet. Risking everything, he eased his arm around her shoulders. "You," he admitted thickly, as he drew Callie to him, "are like the ocean, you know."

Callie felt the strength of his arm go around her, and she acquiesced to Ty's need to hold her. She needed him, too, but was afraid to tell him so. Her hands came to rest against his chest, and their hips lightly touched. As she lifted her head to meet his dark, smoldering gaze, her lips parted. The crash of the surf, the roar of water touching and changing the shifting sand reminded her of herself with Ty Ballard. He was like the restless ocean, and she, the yielding sand beneath the force of it. As she met and drowned in his gaze, her breath caught. In that moment, she knew he was going to kiss her, and nothing had ever seemed so right to her.

Closing her eyes, Callie rose to her tiptoes to meet his descending head. As his mouth swept against her own, she felt his power, felt his strength move against her lips with a certainty that set off a line of explosions through her reeling heart and body. The roughness of his beard, the salty male odor of his skin and caressing warmth of his breath washing across her face all combined to lull her into a world where she was wanted, where she was indeed cherished. His arms moved slowly, easing around her body, pressing her fully against him, and Callie surrendered to Ty, to the safe harbor he was offering her.

The world seemed to melt with each breath she took, with each hungry, exploratory touch of his mouth pressing urgently against her own. With each breath, she met and matched his hunger. As she lifted her lashes slightly, she saw the moonlight touching and caressing his rugged features, bathing both of them in a silvery radiance, as if blessing their kiss. The chilly coolness of the ocean was counterpoint to Ty's warm breath and the heat of his mouth as he caressed her. Lifting her hands, Callie eased them along the planes of his face, delighting in the different textures of him as a man, reveling in the thought of his generous, giving heart. As her fingers tunneled through his thick, dark hair, she felt him tremble against her.

Their breathing was ragged, their mouths devouring each other and their bodies fusing into a heady oneness that left Callie dizzy with need. Gradually, ever so gradually, just as the tide slowly retreated from the sand, Ty eased his mouth away from hers. His eyes were hooded, glittering with unspoken need of her, on every level. Her body tingled hotly as he stroked her shoulders, back and hips. As his mouth drew into a deep smile of satisfaction, her lips lifted in acknowledgment. And when he caressed her hair with his hands, completely absorbed in the touch and texture of her, Callie had never felt more beautiful or more desirable.

"I think," Ty rasped in a gritty voice, "that if we stay out here, we aren't going to get the sleep we need to put us in good stead for tomorrow." Callie's hair was luxurious, and he ached to love her so thoroughly that she'd cry out with utter pleasure. Ty knew he could do that for Callie, but it was something that, if it did happen, was down the road. Just the sparkle in her eyes, the longing he saw in them, told him that she'd enjoyed the kiss just as much as he had. There were a lot of hurdles to overcome, however, and he knew that as never before.

With a small laugh of frustration, Callie said, "I think you're right."

Capturing her face between his hands, Ty looked deeply into her eyes. "But I'm not sorry for anything that happened. Are you?"

She shook her head. "I never gave you a chance," she admitted.

"What do you mean?"

"I thought you were like the pilots I'd had relationships with off and on through the years. I put you in the same mold, but this hearing has shown me you were different."

Ty eased his hands from her face, because if he didn't, he was going to kiss her again. "Now that I understand what fuels your wariness, I can see why you did." He rested his hands on her small shoulders—shoulders that remained strong and proud despite what life had dumped on her.

"I was wary, wasn't I?" She caressed his jaw, thrilled that he enjoyed her touch so much.

"I always wondered why you were like a wild animal around me. You watched me a lot. I could see the distrust in your eyes. It makes sense why you never did trust me. I was an Annapolis graduate, too. I could have been just like the rest of those jerks who had hurt you before."

"But you weren't like them. Over the past week I began to see that."

With a sigh, Ty gripped her hand and they began to walk back toward the parking lot. "Hell of a way to meet, isn't it?"

"Completely unexpected."

Ty drew her to a halt, his face very serious. "Listen, Callie, no matter what happens tomorrow morning, I want our relationship, what we have, to build. I don't want it to end. Do you?"

His honesty was refreshing. It wasn't a line, either—Callie was certain. She squeezed his hand gently. "You've been my still center in this hurricane. You know that, don't you?"

"No, I never realized that's how you saw me."

"You've been there for me since this began. You saved me from a beating I'm sure would've come if you hadn't heard my screams. And when you were ordered to defend me, you could have backed out if you'd really wanted to."

"I did," he admitted, "at first. I was worried what it might do to my career."

"And now?"

"I don't care. I care more about you. You're worth fighting for, worth defending."

A delicious sense, like an ocean tide, moved through Callie. The sincerity in Ty's gaze made her feel solid and prepared for whatever might happen tomorrow morning. "And what if I'm found guilty? You know my reputation will be destroyed. Will you still want to build on what we have?" Callie knew that fraternizing with her after the fact could, indeed, hurt Ty's career. It wasn't fair, but that's how it worked in the navy.

Stepping up to her, Ty brought her into his arms and held her hard against him. "Listen," he breathed against her ear, "I know you're not guilty. I don't care what the board says. I've never walked away from truth in my life, and I'm not about to start now. If they make you a scapegoat, that won't change my feelings for you, Callie. It never will."

The grim atmosphere in the hearing room left Callie's hands sweaty and damp. Commander Newton had several papers in his hand as they reconvened. Callie sat tensely next to Ty. Dr. Marlene Johnson was only a witness and didn't have to remain for the entire session wishing her stomach would unknot just a little.

After kissing Ty last night, she'd realized how much he meant to her. That, combined with the ever-mounting number of phone calls from women in the military who wanted to wish her well, support her, or tell her their equally humiliating and shaming stories, had begun to buoy her in an odd way. Unable to sleep well last night, she'd had more realizations come to her, and she'd begun to see something good growing out of this hearing after all—regardless of the outcome.

"The board," Newton said, his voice echoing through the room, "has diligently looked at all the evidence in this case of sexual harassment. Because of the various testimonies not agreeing with one another, it is impossible to determine who is at fault."

Callie's eyes narrowed, and she felt as if someone had gut-punched her.

"As a result," the commander said, "each officer will have a paper put in his or her personnel jacket detailing this hearing. That is all. Dismissed."

Stunned, Callie stood at attention, as did everyone else as the board rose and left the room. Fury boiled up through her, more heated and more galvanizing than she'd ever experienced. She felt Ty's hand restraining her from moving as, one by one, the pilots filed out. The look of glee on Remington's face sickened her. Relief was written on those of the other pilots. She glared at all of them.

Finally, they were the last two people in the room. Ty slowly turned to Callie. "I'm sorry," he said, shocked by the verdict. "That shouldn't have happened. They had plenty of evidence...."

"Welcome to the real world," Callie whispered fiercely. She was shaking with anger. "I expected it."

Ty studied her pale face and flashing blue eyes. There was such determination in them right now. "I know you did." He rubbed his chin. "I didn't. I mean, they didn't censure Remington at all."

"My career is scuttled. Give them a month and I'll bet they transfer me out of here to some hole-in-the-wall station. Probably Adak, Alaska, if they can get away with it." The derision in her voice didn't escape Ty. Real fear ate at him as he considered her statement.

Placing a hand on her shoulder, he said, "Let's get out of here. I'll take you home, Callie." He felt utterly helpless. So how must she feel, after being railroaded? Worse, Ty knew that tomorrow morning she had to go back to work under Remington's watchful eye.

Callie nodded and walked out of the room and down the passageway. She was grateful that the civilian press had not been allowed on the station during the hearings, but they would be parked on the doorstep of her home. What should she tell them? The truth? Yes.

Ty was silent on the drive to her home. He barely noticed the late-morning blue sky, the golden sun touching the desert landscape. Inwardly, he was hurting for Callie, who remained quiet and contemplative.

"What are you going to do?"

Callie glanced at him, savoring his rugged profile, which she had once feared equaled cruelty. "Go home, dodge the reporters, lock the door and think."

He reached over and gripped her cool, damp hand. "Is there anything I can do?"

"No."

"I can talk to the reporters, too."

She smiled sadly, a fierce longing welling up through her. "If you do that, Ty, your career is as good as dead and you know it."

"So?"

"So, I don't want that to happen. You're happy here. You're a great pilot and teacher."

Squeezing her hand gently, he rasped, "There's a bad taste in my mouth, Callie. I don't like what happened to you. It wasn't right and it wasn't fair. Just because four pilots get together and fabricate a story doesn't make what happened to you right."

"No, it doesn't. But life goes on, and I've got to look long and hard at my career in the navy."

"What do you mean?"

"It's over, Ty. Do you think I can go back to work with Remington? I know what he'll do. He'll harass me verbally even more now that he's gotten away with it—now that he knows the good ol' boys are going to protect him no matter what he does to me or another woman."

She pulled from his grip and rubbed her wrinkled brow. "I never thought something like this would happen to me. After that incident in Annapolis, I worked so hard not to overreact to men hitting on me, harassing me. I just became a ghost, a silent genderless being, praying that if I faded into the background, they'd leave me alone."

A touch of panic ate at Ty. As he turned down the avenue toward Callie's home, he saw many cars and trucks in front of it, representing all the major television stations. Reporters milled around, waiting for her return. Grimly, he parked the car and glanced over at her.

"I'm walking you through that gauntlet."

She smiled a little. "You've always been there for me. Thanks."

The next morning, Ty was at his desk in his small, cluttered office. He sipped hot coffee and tried to pay attention to the curriculum information in front of him. But his head and his heart wouldn't let him forget Callie. How was she doing? Glancing at his watch, he saw it was 0755. At 0800, she had to be over at Intelligence, where he was sure Remington was waiting for her. His hand moved into a fist, and Ty admitted to himself that he wanted to punch the bastard out for what he'd done to her.

Forcing himself to concentrate on his upcoming class, Ty rose. He took the mug of coffee and his lecture notes with him as he moved purposefully down the tiled passageway. The young pilots sat at their desks waiting for him, and the noise died away as he entered the room. As he went to the lectern, they became straight-faced and attentive. It was the last place Ty wanted to be; he wanted to be with Callie to protect her from Remington.

After the lecture, Ty went back to his office to prepare a test for the pilots. To his surprise, Callie, in her light blue summer dress uniform, was waiting for him. He smiled a little and quietly closed the door to his office so that they could have some privacy.

"Hi..."

Callie nodded. "Hi, yourself. I thought I'd come over and tell you what I did."

"Did?" Ty dropped the lecture notes on his desk. He walked over to her and placed his hands on her shoulders. She was very pale, her eyes very dark. "Remington?" he growled.

"I didn't give him a chance. Here, read this," she said, handing him a piece of paper.

Ty released her and stepped back to read the letter. His brows knitted and he glanced up at her. "You're resigning your commission?"

"As of tomorrow morning."

His heart thumped hard in his chest. Callie was leaving the navy. Where would she go? Suddenly, he felt like a greedy miser, unwilling to part with his newfound riches. Handing the paper back to her, he saw a new light in her blue eyes—one of challenge.

"I never expected this."

"Neither did I. Maggie got home last night, and we talked long and hard about it." Callie's mouth lifted in a hint of a smile. "I've had it, Ty. I've taken all I can in the navy in the arena of sexual harassment. I told Maggie everything last night—including what happened to me back at the academy."

"What was her reaction?" Ty leaned against the desk, studying Callie and finding hope in her eyes.

"She cried. Partly out of anger—and partly because she hadn't known." Softly, she added, "We just held each other and cried together. Maggie was hurt because I hadn't told her or Alanna, but she understood why I didn't, too."

"So what led to this resignation?"

With a sigh, Callie moved around his small office. There was a photo of Ty standing proudly beside his F-14 fighter plane, his helmet beneath his arm. He was a warrior in every sense, but a warrior with morals and values—a rarity in today's navy, she thought. Lifting her chin, she held his troubled gaze.

"I showed Maggie all the phone messages, the letters and cards that have been sent to me. She was just amazed. So was I." Callie moved her finger along the smooth, polished surface of the maple desk. "A woman lawyer, Louise Jordan, came over to talk to me last night as well."

"Who is she?"

"She works with the ACLU in San Diego. Maggie met her and liked her, too. Louise has been trying to create a sexual-harassment center in the city. She has permission to create an extension of the American Civil Liberties Union devoted to prosecuting sexual-harassment cases. After reading the newspapers and listening to the television reports, she felt that I would be perfect to help her."

"Oh?" Ty moved over to her. Callie's face was thoughtful with purpose.

"Yes. She made me an offer that I didn't want to refuse, Ty. I'm going to work with Louise to open a center where sexual-harassment data can be collected, public-relations work with the media can take shape and cases can be pursued." She searched his face and saw relief flash across it. "What do you think?"

With a slight grin, Ty asked, "Better yet, how do you feel about it? Is this something you want to do?"

"More than anything," Callie breathed, her voice quavering. "Ty, I've had over fifty phone calls now. Do you know how heartbreaking it is to sit there and hear these women tell me how they've been sexually harassed? How it affects them? No, I've never felt more right about anything."

"So you'll stay here?"

"Yes."

Releasing a long breath, Ty murmured, "I'm glad. I was scared you'd be leaving, moving off somewhere...."

She read between the lines of his admittance. "We really haven't had the time to get to know each other properly, have we?"

With a chuckle, he shook his head. "Not unless you count no time and a lot of pressure as proper. Now that I know you'll be hanging around, I'm making you my priority, if you don't mind."

Heat rushed into her face, but Callie didn't worry about it as joy flowed through her, sweet and hope-filled. "I like being your priority, Commander." Reaching over, she touched his clean-shaven cheek. "I'd better leave. I'm sure you've got work to do."

Ty nodded. "I'm afraid I do. I'd like to take you to dinner, though, Callie. Tonight?"

She smiled a little and met the promise in his dark, narrowed eyes. "Ty, are you sure?"

"About us? Of course I am. Why?"

"Once the navy finds out that I'm actively handling at least fifty sexual-harassment cases that have originated on this station alone, your name will get dragged into it if you see me—or are seen with me."

Touching her flaming red cheek, Ty murmured, "I don't give a damn."

"But—your career . . ."

Just the soft velvet of her skin made him tremble inwardly with need of Callie. He saw the searching, worried look in her blue eyes and managed a deprecating smile. Framing her face between his hands, he whispered, "I learned the hard way about what's really important to me, Callie. I lost a marriage because I put flying before my wife." His voice dropped with feeling. "Never again. I'm not blowing it this time. I've learned my lesson."

Drowning in his gray gaze, Callie felt such incredible hope thread through her that she was speechless. More than anything, she wanted to kiss Ty. It wasn't proper because they were on a military station, but suddenly she didn't care. Placing her hand tentatively on his chest, feeling his reassuring heartbeat beneath her palm, she leaned upward. As she met his mouth, she wasn't disappointed. Ty's arms swept around her, molding her to him, his hunger for her as stunning as it was beautiful. In those moments, all of Callie's fears dissolved in his heat, his giving and taking as their mouths met and clung to each other. His breath became her own, his heart matched rhythm with hers, and she spiraled into a world where she was cherished and loved.

As Callie eased away from Ty, she searched his hooded eyes, which mirrored turbulence and desire. Love? There was that word again. She'd been so gun-shy about ever saying it, much less possibly feeling it. Shaken, but knowing that now they at least had the time, Callie didn't want to look at the revelation too closely. Not yet. As she stepped back and Ty's hand slid down her arm to capture her fingers, Callie realized just how wounded both of them had been by their separate pasts.

"I—I've got to go," she whispered unsteadily.

"Sure..." He wanted to step forward and kiss her again. Kiss her until she was breathless. Her mouth looked soft, beckoning—and Ty had never felt this depth of feeling. "I'll pick you up at 1900?"

"Yes...fine..." She was behaving like a giddy schoolgirl, but Callie savored the feelings and didn't apologize for them. Quietly leaving his office, she walked down the passageway. Her papers would be processed speedily, and she knew that within a week she would be leaving the navy.

As she moved out into the bright, hot sunshine and walked to her car, Callie felt tremendous loads from the past falling away. She had lost her case before the board. She had been made out to be a liar by a group of pilots who had conspired against her. All along, her main concern had been for her career. Now she laughed, the sound carrying across the asphalt parking lot, free and lilting.

In the eyes of the pilot fraternity, she was a loser—someone who had made trouble for them. She was an outsider because she was a woman. What a loss, she thought as she opened her car door to let the accumulated heat out of the vehicle. She was no less intelligent, no less capable than any man, and she knew that. She'd always known it, but because of the incident at Annapolis, she'd demoted herself. Shame was a great leveler, and Callie realized, as she slid into her car, that it had stopped her from standing up and fighting back a lot sooner.

Dr. Lipinski had done her a favor by reporting the incident, she decided as she drove off the station to her home. At the time, she'd been very upset with the doctor's insistence. Now she was on the other side of the storm, and she saw very clearly why the doctor had been adamant.

Feeling better with every mile she put between herself and the station, Callie shifted her thoughts to Ty Ballard. A frown began to form on her brow as she drove up to her home. He was risking his career by continuing to be seen with her. As soon as navy personnel realized that she was going to become a civilian spokesperson on behalf of sexually-harassed navy women, the heat on him would be turned way up.

Her heart jagged at the thought. Climbing out of the car, she moved to the shade and opened the door to her home. More than anything, she didn't want Ty hurt by all of this. Yet the look in his eyes and the promise in his voice told her that hell could erupt and it wouldn't make him back away from knowing her better.

How much her life had changed in one week! She'd been cowering in fear as Lipinski had turned the report in to the legal department. Now she felt revitalized, with a mission that she knew could change the landscape for all women—civilian and military. Compared to her life as an Intelligence officer poring over reconnaissance maps and satellite photos, this was an exciting and challenging change.

Shutting the door, Callie breathed in a huge sigh of relief. At least the reporters were no longer dogging her heels. She'd made some allies among the women reporters, who'd promised her air time when the center opened.

Change, if it was going to come in this sphere, would be made one mincing step at a time. As Callie dropped her purse on the sofa and eased out of her heels, she smiled. Moving into the bedroom, she slipped out of her uniform and threw it in the clothes hamper to be washed. As she went to her closet and opened it, Callie realized that very soon she'd no longer be wearing uniforms. The thought was foreign for a moment as she stood, contemplating what to wear.

As she dressed in a pair of white cotton slacks and a multicolored, short-sleeved blouse, Callie's thoughts rested on Ty. He was a fighter, there was no doubt of that. And more than anything, she liked him for his clear morals, values and principles. Not every navy pilot was like Remington and his group. No, Ty represented the other part of the navy, the part that would begin to work at getting rid of sexual harassment and giving "zero tolerance" some meaning.

Suddenly, Callie was excited as never before. There was fear there, too, but the deep excitement touched her heart and made tears come to her eyes. The next weeks and months were going to be brutal, she knew. Ty had shown his loyalty to her in every way. She only hoped that it wouldn't damage his career.

The phone rang. Frowning, she went to the bedstand and picked up the receiver.

"Hello?"

"Lieutenant Donovan?"

Callie didn't recognize the deep, baritone voice of the man on the other end. "Speaking."

"This is Admiral Winston Burke calling from the Pentagon. Do you have a moment, Lieutenant?"

Shock made Callie stand very still. Admirals didn't make phone calls from the pentagon just to chat. Something was up. Her heart began to pound. "Yes, sir, I do."

Burke cleared his throat. "Good. It came to my attention late this afternoon that you are resigning your commission, Lieutenant. Is that true?"

"Yes, sir, it is."

"Would you reconsider?"

Taking a deep breath, Callie whispered, "No, sir, I wouldn't. Not under the circumstances."

"The board decision?"

"Yes, sir."

"May I be frank with you, Lieutenant Donovan?"

"Yes, sir."

"I've followed your career for nine years, and I like your work. Because of the board decision, I'm initiating a separate investigation on what took place and the attack you suffered, Lieutenant. I don't know what they will find, but I hope it's closer to the truth than what the board allowed in their findings."

Relief flowed through Callie and she released the breath she'd been holding. "You are?"

"Further," Burke went on brusquely, "I'm asking you not to resign your commission until we can investigate this impartially, with an outside team from another naval air station. I guarantee that there will be both women and men on this team. Will you reconsider your decision?"

"Well...I—"

"Lieutenant, I'm ordering the Miramar Personnel Department to hold your resignation until you think about this new development. I want you to realize that not all male officers will protect the 'good ol' boy' system. The navy has invested nine years and almost half a million dollars in your training to do what you do well. I find it reprehensible to lose someone like you over such an issue.''

Callie slowly sat down, dizzy with shock. She tried to think coherently. ''Sir, this is all so sudden. I do have to think about it, and not just because of what happened to me.''

''Excuse me?''

''Sir, there are fifty other women on my station that have contacted me personally to say that they've also been sexually harassed.'' She gulped and went on quickly, knowing it might be the one and only time someone with clout—possibly even the power to change the situation—would listen to her plea. ''To honestly consider withdrawing my resignation, Admiral, I'd have to have your promise to investigate all these women's claims—not just my own. I'm happy to know that someone cares about me and the job I've been doing for the navy, but this situation is much larger, much worse than just my case.'' Her voice lowered with feeling. ''If you're really serious about this, Admiral Burke, you'll launch a station-wide investigation into all the cases, not just mine.''

There was a long moment of silence.

''Is that what it will take for you to stay in the navy, Lieutenant Donovan?''

She heard the tightness in Burke's voice and knew she'd thrown him a curve, but she couldn't apologize for it. ''Yes, sir, that's what it will take.''

''Very well,'' Burke said, ''you have my word on it. Captain Walsh will give you a follow-up phone call in two days with details. In the meantime, my people will alert the station commander that we'll be coming in.''

Callie closed her eyes, relief moving sharply through her. "Thank you, Admiral. I just never expected this . . . help.''

"Not all military men are harassers, Lieutenant. I hope this proves it to you."

"It does, sir."

"Goodbye."

"Goodbye, sir." Callie heard the phone line go dead and she stared at the receiver for a long, long time before gently replacing it in the cradle. Burke was right: not all men in the navy were harassers—or willing to go along with a cover-up. Her heart was optimistic for the first time as she rose and thought of the wonderful dinner she was going to share with Ty. Callie could barely wait to tell him the turn of events.

Chapter Twelve

Ty wanted a quiet restaurant with a lot of privacy, so he'd driven with Callie to The Shadows, a very exclusive, expensive watering hole in La Jolla for the rich and famous of Southern California. Money wasn't the issue tonight; having uninterrupted privacy was. Besides, Callie was worth it, and as he walked into the restaurant, he'd never felt prouder or happier. When she'd shared her latest news with him, he'd been stunned but elated.

Callie practically floated at his side. Her whole world had suddenly been turned inside out by one life-sustaining phone call. And now she had a whole evening alone with Ty Ballard. She looked up and gave him a soft smile. This man in the dark blue suit, white silk shirt and paisley tie was the center of her existence. How handsome Ty looked, recently shaven, his hair dark and emphasizing his rugged features. The gleam in his gray eyes sent her an exquisite message of just how much he liked her. Perhaps, she wondered, even loved her? Callie kept telling herself it was too soon, that love wasn't something that one stumbled upon in such a short space of time.

Feeling very special, she had chosen her clothes carefully, knowing full well that Ty was taking her to a very chic restaurant. She wore a sleeveless black silk dress with a tasteful scoop neck, and over it, a vibrant silk jacket with Aztec-inspired graphics in red, yellow, blue and green. Her small gold earrings and necklace accented the jacket, which was woven with gold metallic threads as well. With black heels and her shining black cap of hair, she felt beautiful indeed. And if she were any judge, Ty thought so, too.

The maître d' showed them to a maroon-leather booth, projecting all the pomp and circumstance of an official military parade. Callie curbed a smile, her arm twined around Ty's as they walked behind the man dressed in a black tuxedo and white shirt. The booth was in the rear of the restaurant, surrounded by a luscious assortment of greenery. The area reminded Callie of a jungle setting, and as she sat down next to Ty, she smiled at him. After a brief flurry of activity by the vanguard of waiters, the silence was broken only by soft piano music drifting from another region of the large restaurant.

"Quite a place," Ty commented wryly.

"Really."

"Does it make you uncomfortable?"

Callie shook her head. "I guess I can put up with the pretense as long as the food is good."

"And the company is good."

"Touché."

Ty reached over and captured her hand. "I wanted a quiet, secluded spot, not a place where the maître d' and his staff have their noses in the air."

Laughing softly, Callie responded to his touch, an ache centering deep within her. "I won't take them seriously if you won't."

Rallying, he grinned. "I like your flexibility." Sobering a bit, he lifted her hand and kissed the back of it, her skin fragrant with perfume. "I know the good news about Burke, but tell me, how did it go today over at Personnel when you turned in your resignation? I'm just curious."

Sitting back, Callie said, "Strained and tense. Commander Waring, who is the head of Personnel, gave me my departing interview and studiously wrote out my reasons for resigning my commission. Most of the time he had a wrinkled brow, and he was sweating a lot."

With a shake of his head, Ty muttered, "I wonder if he made the call to the admiral at the Pentagon?"

"I don't know," Callie said thoughtfully.

"I'm glad to see the navy isn't willing to lose someone who is invaluable to them. Look at the time and money they've poured into your education. You'd think it would tip the balance."

"Maybe it did," Callie said softly. "This change means I'm going to have to prepare files on all the cases I want to pursue next week when Captain Walsh calls. Something good has come out of this after all, Ty."

With a blinding smile, he nodded. He'd ordered a bottle of chardonnay, and it was brought and the crystal goblets filled. Left alone, he handed Callie her glass and touched the rim of his own to it.

"Here's to a brave new world where you are going to make a difference," he toasted.

Callie met and held his warm gaze across the wineglasses. "Yes," she whispered. As she sipped the slightly oak-flavored wine, she ruminated that Ty had made a huge, important difference in her world. Setting the goblet aside, she turned to him.

"Do you think you'll be penalized because of me and what is going to happen on the station?"

With a shake of his head, Ty said, "I don't think so. I don't think I'm going to get any hassle."

Moistening her lips, she said, "But what if our relationship continues? Up until now, no one knew about it. Since I'm going to stay in, they'll know about it at the station."

"What do you mean, if?"

Callie gave an embarrassed shrug. "Well..."

"No 'well' about it," Ty growled. He tightened his grip on her hand. "I'm in for the long haul. How about you?" His breath was suspended as he met her shadowed blue eyes.

The unparalleled warmth and monitored strength of his hand around hers made Callie choke up for a moment. "Everything happened so fast, Ty. We didn't even like each other at first...."

"That was my fault. I liked you the moment I saw you there in the parking lot. Things got fouled up because my commander ordered me to defend you. I admit, at first I didn't want to do it, but later, I was glad I'd been ordered into the fray."

"I'm glad, too," Callie said softly. "You showed me that there is one officer in the navy with morals more important than his concern about his career."

"Sweetheart," Ty whispered as he placed his arm around her shoulders and drew her against him, "there are a lot of fine officers in the navy who are exactly like me. Admiral Burke certainly is. Remington and his bunch are in the minority."

"But I never thought Andy Clark would lie like that, Ty. I know I didn't know him well, but he seemed like a really decent guy—nothing like Remington."

Ty sighed and shook his head in answer. A long moment later he pressed a kiss to her puzzled brow. "You know something?"

Languishing beneath his care, her heart starting to pound a little crazily, Callie whispered, "What?"

"Tonight is ours for as long as you want us to be together."

Closing her eyes, she rested against Ty, feeling happier than she even remembered being. "All night?"

"If that's what you want, Callie."

Stretching upward, she pressed a soft kiss against his very male mouth. "Yes," she whispered against him, "all night."

Ty tried to contain his surprise as he drove into the parking lot of Callie's apartment complex. She'd wanted to come home to change clothes and pick up some clothes, since they planned to spend the day at the beach after waking up at his place tomorrow morning. There, standing next to Callie's car, was Lieutenant Clark.

"Ty..." Callie stared at the navy officer as they drove up alongside her car. "What's Andy doing here at this time of night?"

"I don't know." Frowning, Ty shut off the engine and climbed out. Callie left the car and walked over to the officer.

Callie tried to handle her sudden, jittery feelings as she stopped within a few feet of Clark. He was still dressed in his summer white uniform, nervously twisting the hat in his hands.

"What do you want?" Callie demanded huskily. She felt Ty's hand come to rest on her shoulder, felt the protection he gave her.

"I—uh, I heard scuttlebutt on the station late today that you were resigning your commission, Lieutenant Donovan."

Callie wasn't able to deny that, since Admiral Burke had sworn her to secrecy. "News gets around fast, doesn't it?" She saw the sweat standing out on Clark's brow and noted the anxiety evident not only in the way he was moving his hat in his hands, but in the darting quality in his eyes.

"Damn...I mean, I'm sorry. I didn't realize..." He stopped, his voice dropping into a guilt-ridden rasp. "I hoped it wasn't true."

"The board found me guilty of something I didn't do. Why would anyone stay in an organization like that?"

Wincing, Clark looked toward Ty and then back to her. "God, I never meant for it to go this far. I—I just thought—"

"What?" Ty demanded tightly. "That if you threw in with Remington and his boys you'd be nice and safe? No hassle? No career worries?"

"Yeah, something like that," Clark muttered. He opened his hands in Callie's direction. "Look, I feel bad about this."

"But not so bad as to tell the truth?" Ty demanded.

"Please," Callie begged, "let Andy finish what he's trying to tell us."

Bridling, Ty snapped his mouth shut, his anger rising by the second.

"I had that coming," Clark said. "You've got to understand something, Lieutenant Donovan. I never thought it would go this far. I really didn't. I'm sorry you've resigned. That wasn't right, either." Helplessly, he shrugged, and his voice became scratchy with tension. "I've got a wife and two kids to support. If I told the truth and sided with you, I knew that my career was down the tubes. There's a recession in our country. A deep one. And even though I'm a pilot, I might not get a job—it's that bad. Please...I couldn't risk my family to testify for you. Can you understand?"

Callie closed her eyes, feeling the pilot's guilt and pain over his flawed decision. She lifted her lashes and held Clark's anguished gaze. "Sometimes," she choked, "we all have to do things we don't want to do, Lieutenant Clark. I'm just sorry you couldn't put your values ahead of your pocketbook."

"But it was my family," he entreated. "If it were just me, I'd have told the truth for you. I—I didn't want my entire family punished."

Unable to contain himself any longer, Ty punched his index finger in Clark's direction. "There's no easy answer on this, Clark, and you know it. But you're an academy graduate just like me. You're bound by a higher law to always tell the truth and not participate in any kind of cover-up. I don't care what your reason. You were taught for four years to tell the truth no matter what. How do you think I feel about this? I'm a ring-knocker, too. A part of the brotherhood. Do you think I respect any of you for your lies?"

Wincing, Clark took a step back, unable to look Ty in the eyes. "Don't you think that hasn't bothered me, Commander? I sat in that board hearing, my stomach in knots. I wanted to puke." Lifting his head, he gave Callie an anguished look of apology. "I know you understand, Lieutenant Donovan."

"I understand," Callie said brokenly, "but it doesn't make it right. It never will."

"I tried to rationalize it. I spent sleepless nights looking at all the angles. I have a family to support and feed. You're single, and you don't have a family to worry about. I'm up for lieutenant commander, and I didn't want my chances of getting the higher rank and the pay that comes with it screwed with this board hearing. My youngest daughter has a learning disability, and with the extra pay we were going to be able to get her to a special teaching facility." Looking away, Clark tried to hold back his emotions by compressing his lips for a moment. Finally, he looked back at Callie. "I'm sorry. I feel like hell about this. I always will. What I did wasn't right. I just tried to make the best decision for all concerned."

"You don't rationalize the truth, Clark. Not ever! You didn't look at all the angles, either, buddy. Did you know that Callie was up for lieutenant commander, too? How the hell do you know where the money she makes goes? Maybe it's to a sick parent, or another member of her family. The point is—" Ty grabbed Clark by his shirtfront "—you made some very lousy, selfish rationalizations that concerned you, not her." With a growl, he released the officer. "You make me ashamed to be an academy graduate."

Callie choked back the desire to tell Clark that she'd decided not to resign. He looked like a beaten dog. His conscience was eating him alive, there was no doubt. He was a tortured man in every sense of the word. She felt Ty's hand on her arm, gently urging her to come with him. Woodenly, Clark straightened his uniform and put the hat back on his head. He gave Callie a woeful look turned and walked back to his car.

Ty was breathing hard and trying to control his anger. After Clark drove away, he released a ragged sigh. "You okay?"

Callie turned and moved into his arms. Ty's face was glowering with fury. "I'm okay," she said and reached up and touched his cheek.

"I can't believe he lied," Ty breathed. "Not when he's being eaten alive by it."

"Water under the bridge," Callie whispered. She allowed her hands to remain on his chest, the beat of his heart palpable beneath her palms. "Clark has to live with his decision—no matter how much he tried to rationalize it."

"Well, he'll get a second chance to square with his conscience. I'm sure Burke's team will interview him again in their investigation. But I hope like hell he has sleepless nights for the rest of his life over what he did to you."

There really were no easy answers, Callie decided. A part of her, the objective side, understood Clark's agonizing decision in favor of his family. It was obvious he worried greatly over his daughter with the learning disorder. As Ty walked with her into her apartment, she felt only sadness, not anger or betrayal.

"At least," Callie said as she switched on one of the living-room lamps, "Clark had the courage to come and tell me to my face. I don't expect Remington or the other two to do that."

Ty shrugged out of his jacket and let it drop on the back of the sofa. "I think he came over here to try to somehow make himself feel less guilty," he said as he loosened the tie. Now, more than ever, he wanted to love Callie. He wanted to show her the good side to a man; she'd been seeing the underside for too long. Moving over to where she stood next to the lamp, the light softly outlining her strained features, he placed his hands on her shoulders.

"I'm sorry it had to happen tonight. I wanted things to be perfect after all the hell you'd gone through," he said, gently massaging her shoulders. As Callie lifted her chin and stared up into his eyes, Ty felt a joy suffuse him, like rolling thunder through the very heart of his body, his soul.

"I'm not sorry," Callie whispered, and stood up on tiptoe to place a warm, inviting kiss on his grim mouth. She felt the tension in Ty, the anger, but she also felt his lips melt and become willing beneath her gentle assault. Right now, all she wanted to do was focus on something good and clean, something that was honest—and her feelings for him were exactly that. As his arms slid around her, capturing her against him, she smiled against his mouth and surrendered to his male strength coupled with exquisite tenderness as his mouth took hers.

With a groan of raging need, Ty leaned down and swept Callie into his arms. Her own arms settled around his shoulders, and he felt the moistness of her breath as she sighed, resting her head against his as he carried her down the hall to her bedroom. Nudging the door open, he stepped inside.

Nothing could have prepared Ty for the ethereal beauty of her bedroom. As he stood there with Callie in his arms, warm and soft against him, he saw a four-poster bed with chiffon drapery across the top of it, tied in languorous folds to each of the posts. The gauzy pink curtains in the window were equally feminine. Large green plants, almost small trees, were nestled in two of the corners. A small round table covered with a flowery cloth compounded the Victorian decor.

Smiling down at her, he said, "Your bedroom shows a whole other side of you."

Callie returned his smile, never more happy than in this moment in his arms. "I think it mirrors the woman in me," she whispered. "The one that doesn't have to wear a military uniform."

"You're like that tidal pool we saw the other night. There are so many facets to you," he murmured, and walked over to the bed. The thick quilt was colored with huge pink, white and red peonies on a green-and-ivory background. The pink chiffon hung in huge, loose folds, and moved slightly as he laid her on the bed, then joined her. Moonlight filtered through the window, lending a soft radiance to the room. As Ty pushed off his shoes and they dropped to the thick, dusky carpet, he felt Callie's hands move upward across his shirt. His skin prickled where her fingers glided across the silky fabric to begin unbuttoning his shirt.

The very male smile Ty gave her as she pulled the shirt away from his chest made Callie feel bold— beautiful. She felt an incredible sense of wonder laced with joy as he began to remove her Aztec-design jacket. His white silk shirt fell to the carpet with it. The simple black dress had a zipper, and he gently turned her away from him and began to slowly pull it downward. Every few inches the zipper would stop, and she would feel his hot breath and then a soft kiss on her back as the dress peeled open beneath his coaxing. Each kiss was like a searching quest—hot, slow and exquisite. Callie could only sit there, her breath coming in ragged sighs as Ty worked the zipper downward.

"You're so beautiful," he rasped as he slid his hands beneath the dress and pulled it away from her skin. Each time he caressed her with a kiss, he felt her gasp, felt her tense, in the way of a woman enjoying each heated touch he bestowed upon her. Just removing Callie's dress was a delicious adventure to him. And her lacy black lingerie underneath made him smile with appreciation. The luster burning in her eyes told him that she not only welcomed his touch, but desired more of it and him.

As Ty leaned down and captured her awaiting mouth, he slid his hand beneath her and eased the black, lacy bra from her. His hand trembling, he barely cupped her small breast and felt her arch toward him with a soft gasp of pleasure. His body thrummed, hard and on fire as she melted against him beneath his caresses. Her fingers dug frantically into his shoulders, kneading his taut muscles, begging him in the silent language of love to continue his exploration of her.

Moving his mouth strongly against her wet, soft lips, Ty realized in some distant compartment of his mind and heart that he did love Callie. When and how it had happened was beyond him, but he recognized that fierce, all-consuming feeling for the second time in his life. Humbled by the emotion sweeping like a tidal wave through him, he felt her cool fingers move with trembling certainty down across his chest and torso. Callie had gone through so much alone that he concentrated on tempering his hunger in lieu of her needs. Love was about pleasing, about sharing, not selfishly taking for one's own pleasure. Lifting his head as he broke the long, hot kiss, he saw the joy reflected in her half-closed eyes. He felt like the strongest, most powerful man in the world at that moment.

Time merged with the moonlight. Ty's inciting touch slowly explored each curve, each valley of her. Callie had tried to give him equal pleasure, but somehow he'd turned the table, transforming her needs into a raging, out-of-control fire that burned hotly within her for him alone. They lay naked together, and she gloried in the strength and hardness of his body against hers. There was such suppleness to Ty, such power, that she trembled with a hunger she'd never known before as he continued to move his hands in provocative, teasing caresses.

The moment his lips settled on the peak of her taut breast, Callie became mindless, moaning his name and clamoring for more of him. The moistness of his breath, the strength of his body meeting hers, the growl that rumbled through him as he merged into her, made her cry out in joy. There was such tenderness as he took her, becoming one with her. At first he held very still, until he was sure that she had adjusted to him, and then, with a smile in his eyes, he began to move slowly, rhythmically, just as the ocean moves in and out from the restless, sandy shore. Each surge created more fire. Each plunge made her gasp for a deepening, a joining with him. The perspiration mingled and merged, slid and became molten until she felt the oneness, the mindlessness consume her. The powerful surge exploded deep within her, spreading outward in waves and taking her breath away. In those exquisite moments, Callie clung to Ty, understanding as never before what love was really all about. She felt him holding her tightly, his head pressed against hers, his breathing ragged and thick.

Just as she thought there could never be more beauty than this with loving someone, Callie felt him stiffen and grow taut against her. His embrace tightened like steel bands around her, nearly crushing the breath from her, flowing into her as the ocean flows inexorably across the golden sand, making it one with the water for that brief moment. Glorying in his release, in the animal growl that shook through her, Callie smiled.

Easing Callie down on the bed moments later, Ty was struck by the softness of her smile. Her lips were parted, the corners gently lifted upward. He nearly cried because that smile had transferred to her lovely blue eyes, now filled with love. He didn't want to ever leave her. The feeling was so right, so overwhelming, that all he could do was absorb her look and take it within himself. Ty had never experienced such an intensity, a peeling back of his raw, primal feelings as he had with Callie. Moving slowly, he kept his weight on his elbows as he lay above her. Her breasts lightly touched his chest with each breath she took. Each stroke of her hands on his damp back made him wildly aware of just how much he wanted her all over again.

With his hands, he pushed back her tangled black hair, damp and stuck to her skin. Both of them were breathing erratically, and he pressed his head against hers, their noses touching. Smiling a little, Ty whispered, "You're like the ocean—wild, primitive and beautiful."

Stirring slightly, Callie raised her lashes and drowned in the brilliant diamond color of his eyes. "I've never thought of myself like that."

"A luminescent pearl stolen from an oyster," he continued thickly. "One of a kind—my kind," and he rolled off her, then pulled her back into his arms.

Content simply to lie against him, her arm across his broad chest, Callie smiled sleepily. "I never realized you were such a poet."

"I didn't, either," Ty chuckled. "I guess it's you. You bring it out in me." He reached over and brought the quilt across them so that she wouldn't get chilled. The tousled hair made Callie look more girl than woman, but her lips were well kissed, and the lingering desire in her eyes only made him more aware than ever of wanting to be the only man in her life.

Joy rippled through Callie like tiny wavelets as she closed her eyes, held within Ty's embrace. This man was not offended by her strength as a woman. Just the opposite. He had reveled in her assertiveness in initiating their lovemaking. How different Ty was from the others. With a sigh, Callie was thankful that she had drawn him into her life, because Ty enriched it in ways she'd never known could exist. Sleep touched her, and without another word, Callie surrendered and sank into a blissful world where only happiness existed. Tomorrow was a new start to her life, and she could hardly wait to awaken the next morning with Ty at her side to begin living it.

The ocean breeze wafted strands of Callie's recently washed hair into her face momentarily. Ty had the camera and snapped the picture just as she reached down into a tidal pool to touch a bright orange starfish with her index finger. Dressed in a tangerine short-sleeved blouse and a pair of loose, well-worn jeans rolled up to her knees, and barefoot, she presented a heart-wrenching picture through the lens. If he was lucky, the camera might be able to catch the moment, but Ty had already burned the image into his heart forever.

The tangy salt air blended with the dampness of the sand. The morning sun sent slanting rays across the glassy ocean, and gulls wheeled and turned above them, hoping for handouts. Ty had coaxed the camera out of Callie's hands so that he might take some shots. His photos would be less than artful, but he wanted pictures of her doing what she loved so much to do: in touch with the ocean's beauty and power. Beneath their clothes they wore their swimsuits, and when it got warm enough, around noon, they would swim in the green-and-blue waters of the Pacific—together.

Callie lifted her head, smiling as she picked up the starfish and held it up so that Ty would get his photograph. He was kneeling on the black, smooth surface of the rocks, both hands on the camera. The breeze swirled and played around them, pulling at his yellow polo shirt and the loose denim jacket he wore with his jeans. Today he looked dangerously beautiful in a very male way, Callie thought. He dropped the camera, allowing it to hang from his neck, then rose like a lithe jaguar and made his way toward her. There was such animal grace in him, and it made Callie go hot with longing all over again.

Gently, she placed the starfish back in the tidal pool. Ty crouched by her side, and she relished his closeness. Looking up, she felt herself surrounded by his warmth.

"What do you say we hit that picnic basket we packed and break into the thermos of hot coffee?"

She smiled. "I could use a cup, too." And she held out her hand to him as he rose beside her.

Ty wasn't satisfied with just Callie's hand. He pulled her hard against him and encircled her with his arms. "Mmm," he growled as he pressed his head against hers and held her tightly, "this warms me even more than that cup of coffee."

Giggling, Callie drew away just enough to place a molten kiss on his smiling mouth. Nothing could have prepared her for his returning kiss, which made her feel fire explode unexpectedly to life throughout her tingling, aching body. His mouth was confident, sharing and searching with an intense heat that made her melt and fuse against him. The roar of the ocean grew dim against the beat of his heart pounding raggedly against her own. The salty air mingled with his male scent, drawn deeply into her lungs as if it were an aphrodisiac. The cries of the gulls, sharp and serrating, echoed the cry within her heart for the love she felt so keenly for Ty alone.

As he broke their fiery kiss, his eyes burning with a desire that made her tremble, Callie knew it was too soon to talk of love. But they had the time now to explore each other at a slower, more delicious pace, and that was all right with her. She didn't feel the need to tell him of her love; she could show it to him, share it with him in a hundred small but important ways. Yet, as she held his smoldering gray gaze, she knew without a doubt that Ty loved her, too. The discovery was wonderful and exhilarating.

"Come on," he rasped thickly as he released her, one arm remaining around her waist, "let's get that coffee. If I don't, I'm going to get you."

With a grin, Callie chortled and nodded. She made a point of looking around the shining black lava rocks that contained the tidal pools. "I think we'd shock the tourists, don't you?"

Ty grudgingly looked around in turn. More and more tourists were coming to explore the same area. "I guess you're right," he muttered unhappily.

Callie was content to walk with Ty, his arm thrown carelessly about her shoulder as they slogged barefoot through the damp sand. They had laid out their red plaid blanket a quarter of a mile farther up the beach and placed the wicker picnic basket upon it.

As they sat together, cups of hot coffee in hand, watching the morning ease away the dampness and chill, Callie smiled. They faced the ocean, and the black-and-white seagulls landed in force around them, begging for scraps of food.

"They're such beggars," Ty said as he reached into the basket for a box of chips.

"And you're such a softy," Callie laughed. She watched as he scattered the chips to the gulls, which raced toward them. Some of the younger gulls were gray, the older ones snow white with black edging on their wings and tails.

Tossing some of the chips in a wide arc so many of the gulls would get some, Ty glanced down at Callie. Her face was flushed, and he'd never seen such happiness burning in her blue eyes. "Didn't you think I had a soft side?" he teased.

"Not at first I didn't. I thought you were very tough and very hard, Commander Ballard." And then, more softly, she added, "You scared me because you reminded me of the past, of what had happened to me at the academy."

With a nod, Ty closed the box and put it away. The fight between the gulls was fierce, and they took to the air with their scraps. Circling his arm around Callie's shoulders, he rested his cheek against her hair. "Are you scared now?"

"Of you? No." Callie raised her head a bit and met his gaze.

"What of the future?"

"Yes, I'm scared—but hopeful. I feel I can make a difference, Ty." She chewed on her lip. "I still worry that it will somehow hurt your career."

"Naw, not a chance." He gave her a boyish smile of reassurance. "Let's talk about something more important."

"Okay. What?"

"Us."

Callie studied him from beneath her black lashes, her heart beating a bit harder in her breast. "What about us?" she asked softly.

"I like what we have. Do you?"

"Very much."

"We've come a long way in a hurry, Callie. Maybe too fast."

"Maybe," she agreed slowly. "But I'm not sorry about it. About loving you last night."

"No?"

"No. Never."

He smiled a little. "That's one of the many things I like about you, Callie Donovan—you're not a wishy-washy person. You have opinions, and you stick by them, no matter what. You're very clear about where you are with yourself, and you don't mince words."

She stared deeply into his eyes. "What about you, Ty? Are you sorry about last night? Was it too soon?"

Caressing her red cheek, Ty gave her a very masculine smile. "Sweetheart, last night was like a dream to me. How can I be sorry it happened or when it happened? No, if anything, I want more of you, Callie, not less. I'm hungry for you in every way possible. I find myself wishing I could apply for leave and spend thirty unbroken, private days just exploring you, your heart, your mind." He leaned down and worshipped her parted lips, savoring the taste of sweet, creamy coffee on them. "I want to explore that hot, fiery body of yours, too."

With a little laugh, Callie set her cup aside and placed her arms across his broad shoulders. "You're so sensual, Ty Ballard. Almost like hot, flowing lava."

"We're not bad together, are we?"

She smiled at his preening. "Not bad at all."

Moving his hands across her sleek black cap of hair, he pressed his brow against hers. "I like what we have," he told her in a low, gritty tone. "I want to keep it. I want to explore it with you. This isn't a casual relationship for me, Callie."

She closed her eyes and simply absorbed his caressing strokes across her hair. "I was never any good at casual loving, either. I've made a lot of mistakes in my past relationships, Ty."

"Look at me. You think I'm going to judge you?" He snorted softly and said, "Neither of us is perfect, but I think together we're a pretty good team. Don't you?"

Callie eased away enough to frame his face with her hands. "Pretty good?" she quavered. "I know knights on white horses aren't supposed to exist anymore, but you do for me. You have integrity, Ty."

With a sigh, he nodded. "I know our world is moving so fast right now that it's tough to keep up with all the changes. I don't think they should have thrown knights on white horses out with everything else. We can learn from our past, but we don't have to abandon it.''

''I agree.''

''In a way,'' he murmured as he grazed her cheek, ''you're a champion, a knight on a charger, too.''

''Oh?''

''Sure. You're going to be a champion to other women who have suffered what you've gone through. You're turning defeat into victory, and sweetheart, I can't begin to tell you how much I admire your courage.'' Ty looked deeply into her eyes, wanting badly to impress on her just how much he admired her bravery.

Shaken by his insight, his commitment to her and to the new goals she'd just established, Callie sniffed. ''When you get trampled there's only one way to go—up.''

''That's true,'' Ty said, ''but how many women would have fought back? You can be a good role model for them, Callie. And I really believe you'll help them to help themselves.''

''I want to get the laws changed, Ty.''

''There's no reason you can't learn how to lobby and get it done. I'll help you all I can.''

Startled, Callie saw his mouth curve upward. ''You mean that?'' she asked wonderingly.

''Sure. If you think I enjoyed seeing those men intimidate and hurt you, you're wrong! No man who's secure in his own masculinity would like it, Callie. We've got some bad apples in our barrel, but there are plenty of men out there who will be on our side. Wait and see.''

Touched and unable to say anything, because her love for him was as boundless as the ocean that embraced them, Callie nodded. The fact that Ty had used the word *us* said more than she dared hope. Sliding her fingertips across his recently shaven cheek, she said in an aching whisper, "We've got the time now."

"Yes," Ty murmured, capturing her lips beneath his, "from now until forever, sweetheart."

* * * * *

A Note from the Author

I felt very proud to be asked to take part in the That Special Woman! program. My editors know my fondness for writing novels that emphasize women and their wonderful strengths, intelligence, creativity and courage. And I think my readers know where I stand on the issues of women and their rights. I've always supported women in every way.

Navy Lieutenant Callie Donovan faces a challenge while in a very male-dominated career position. She gets put up against a wall, and when she's forced to, she fights back. I don't think women like to fight; we'd rather work things out peaceably, but more and more we must stand up for our own integrity. I believe Lieutenant Callie Donovan has the "right stuff"—just as all women do. None of us should be treated disrespectfully or without integrity.

Lindsay McKenna

He staked his claim…

HONOR BOUND

by
New York Times
Bestselling Author

previously published under the pseudonym Erin St. Claire

As Aislinn Andrews opened her mouth to scream, a hard
hand clamped over her face and she found herself face-
to-face with Lucas Greywolf, a lean, lethal-looking
Navajo and escaped convict who swore he wouldn't hurt
her— *if* she helped him.

Look for HONOR BOUND at your favorite
retail outlet this January.

Only from…

Silhouette

where passion lives. SBHB

**Relive the romance...
Harlequin and Silhouette
are proud to present**

by Request™

A program of collections of three complete novels by the most requested authors with the most requested themes. Be sure to look for one volume each month with three complete novels by top name authors.

In January: **WESTERN LOVING**   Susan Fox
                                    JoAnn Ross
                                    Barbara Kaye

Loving a cowboy is easy—taming him isn't!

In February: **LOVER, COME BACK!**   Diana Palmer
                                        Lisa Jackson
                                        Patricia Gardner Evans
It was over so long ago—yet now they're calling, "Lover, Come Back!"

In March: **TEMPERATURE RISING**   JoAnn Ross
                                      Tess Gerritsen
                                      Jacqueline Diamond

Falling in love—just what the doctor ordered!

Available at your favorite retail outlet.

REQ-G3

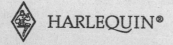

Christmas Classics

Share in the joys of finding happiness and exchanging the ultimate gift—love—in full-length classic holiday treasures by two bestselling authors

JOAN HOHL
EMILIE RICHARDS

Available in December at
your favorite retail outlet.

Only from **ꟍ Silhouette**® where passion lives.

When the only time you have for yourself is…

STOLEN *moments* ™

Christmas is such a busy time—with shopping, decorating, writing cards, trimming trees, wrapping gifts.…

When you do have a few *stolen moments* to call your own, treat yourself to a brand-new *short* novel. Relax with one of our Stocking Stuffers— or with all six!

Each STOLEN MOMENTS title is a complete and original contemporary romance that's the perfect length for the busy woman of the nineties! Especially at Christmas…

And they make perfect **stocking stuffers,** too! (For your mother, grandmother, daughters, friends, co-workers, neighbors, aunts, cousins—all the other women in your life!)

Look for the STOLEN MOMENTS display in December

STOCKING STUFFERS:

HIS MISTRESS Carrie Alexander
DANIEL'S DECEPTION Marie DeWitt
SNOW ANGEL Isolde Evans
THE FAMILY MAN Danielle Kelly
THE LONE WOLF Ellen Rogers
MONTANA CHRISTMAS Lynn Russell

HSM2

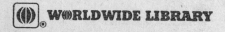 **W⊕RLDWIDE LIBRARY** ®

Also available by popular author

LINDSAY McKENNA

Silhouette Special Edition®

#09649	•DAWN OF VALOR	$2.95	☐
#09667	•NO QUARTER GIVEN	$3.25	☐
#09673	•THE GAUNTLET	$3.25	☐
#09679	•UNDER FIRE	$3.25	☐
#09721	†RIDE THE TIGER	$3.29	☐
#09727	†ONE MAN'S WAR	$3.39	☐
#09733	†OFF LIMITS	$3.39	☐
#09818	*HEART OF THE WOLF	$3.50	☐
#09824	*THE ROGUE	$3.50	☐
#09830	*COMMANDO	$3.50	☐

•Love & Glory miniseries
•Women of Glory miniseries
†Moments of Glory miniseries
*Morgan's Mercenaries miniseries

(limited quantities available on certain title)

TOTAL AMOUNT	$
POSTAGE & HANDLING	$
($1.00 for one book, 50¢ for each additional)	
APPLICABLE TAXES**	$ _____
<u>**TOTAL PAYABLE**</u>	$ _____
(Send check or money order—please do not send cash)	

To order, complete this form and send it, along with a check or money order
for the total above, payable to Silhouette Books, to: **In the U.S.:** 3010 Walden
Avenue, P.O. Box 9077, Buffalo, NY 14269-9077; **in Canada:** P.O. Box 636,
Fort Erie, Ontario, L2A 5X3.

Name: _____

Address: _____ City: _____

State/Prov.: _____ Zip/Postal Code: _____

**New York residents remit applicable sales taxes.
Canadian residents remit applicable GST and provincial taxes.

LMcBACK1

Silhouette ®